"They put you in a hospital and stick tubes down your nose," Emily said. "That's what my father told me. He said they strap you to a bed and feed you through your nose until you're fat."

"No one's going to do that," I told her. "It's revolting. Plus, it's crazy. He's just trying to scare you."

"That's what he said," Emily insisted. "I swear. He wants to fatten me up. Like a pig. Like a turkey, for Thanksgiving. Like a big fat blimp." We were still sitting in the coffee shop. The waitress had long ago removed my empty plate and though Emily had stopped crying, she looked like she could start again at any minute. Either that or explode. "He hates my mother for being fat and then he wants me to be just like her. He said if I don't start eating, he'll put me in a mental hospital where they tie you up until you eat."

I AM AN ARTICHOKE

LUCY FRANK

LAUREL-LEAF BOOKS

Published by
Bantam Doubleday Dell Books for Young Readers
a division of
Bantam Doubleday Dell Publishing Group, Inc.
1540 Broadway
New York, New York 10036

ISBN: 0-440-21990-6

RL: 5.1

Reprinted by arrangement with Holiday House, Inc.

Printed in the United States of America

November 1996

10 9 8 7 6 5 4 3 2 1

OPM

I AM
AN
ARTICHOKE

CHAPTER 1

I prayed a lot when I was little. Not to God specifically, and not in the usual places. My family wasn't into that. We have this huge bush at the corner of the house and when no one was around, that's where I'd go. I'd kneel in front of it with my eyes closed and my hands pressed together and pray for things, like to be returned to my real family (this is when I was much younger and still believed there'd been some mix-up when I was born), or for my sister to disappear, or just for them to be nicer to me. Those prayers never worked, but I got enough of the small, everyday stuff I asked for to keep me hoping. Then, for some reason I gave up on it, till recently, when my life was really getting to me, and I started doing it again. Not kneeling down or anything. Praying to a rhododendron is too bizarre even for me. Just sort of walking past and whispering, "Please, get me out of here."

I'm sure it was those prayers that started everything.

We got the call a few days after school ended: my mother's friend knew someone in New York City who needed a mother's helper for the summer. My older sister, Shelley, had no interest. She had so many friends, plus her cheerleading clinic, plus her boyfriend, Bart. My mother thought it was a bad idea to work for somebody we didn't know. Plus, she said, New York City was not an appropriate place for a fifteen-year-old girl. That in itself made me think the job was worth pursuing. Then she said I was temperamentally unsuited to being a mother's helper. "A mother's helper has to like helping people, Sarah," she said.

That clinched it. "Let me at least meet the lady," I said. And after much wrangling, my mother called back and arranged for an appointment the following day.

The next morning I was up at six, so I could ride into the city with my father. I was pretty nervous. I'd been to New York City hundreds of times—we live only an hour away—but never by myself and, obviously, never for an interview.

"Well, Sarah," my mother said, "I hope you won't be as surly with Mrs. Friedman as you've been around here lately." Giving me no credit whatsoever for (a) being a basically likable human being, or (b) knowing how to act. She can't seem to accept that I'm not like Shelley. Shelley is a People Person. Shelley thinks her life is perfect. Shelley, ever since she was thirteen, has insisted that everyone spell her name Shelli. I refuse. In fact, when she's being particularly phony, I call her Shirley. I may not be a People Person, but at least no one says about me, "Isn't she *adorable!*" I'd rather be called loathsome or odious or unspeakable. That, at least, has dignity. Anyway, after that "surly" comment, I was super-pleasant all through breakfast, so that by the time we left, I felt like I'd put in a full day's work.

My father spent the train ride reading the *Wall Street Journal.* I spent it trying to check out what people thought of me. The train conductor seemed to like me well enough. He looked right in my face and smiled as he punched my ticket. I had a whole little conversation with some friend of my father's. And when we got up to my father's office, the secretaries all fussed over me. So I couldn't have been that negative, to use another of my mother's favorite words.

But what if this Mrs. Friedman hated me, I thought, as I left my father's office and walked toward the bus.

What if her kids started crying when they saw me, or her dog took one look at me and began to snarl? It would be humiliating to come home and admit to everyone I didn't get the job. This poem kept running through my head, this poem I wrote when I was in the eighth grade. It began, "I am an artichoke," about having to peel through all these outer layers to find the real me. The teacher liked it so much he read it to the class. But then kids started going around saying, in these bombastic voices, "I am an eggplant," "I am a rutabaga," and for a long time afterward, part of me went through this whole thing of feeling ridiculous and sorry I'd ever written it and thinking, that's the last poem I'll ever write. But then, another part said, what do they know? So now I don't show anyone my poems.

I didn't want to be too early, so I stopped by a guy selling sunglasses on the street and tried on about a hundred pairs until I found some for eight dollars that looked good. Then I walked into this fancy croissant and frozen yogurt shop and bought three muffins. I hadn't planned to buy any, but they were so big and delicious-looking, I couldn't help myself. I ate the raspberry-amaretto muffin on the uptown bus, which was kind of hard standing crammed up against all these business types with briefcases, and because the raspberry jam kept squirting out the sides. But it was really good. I was sorry to see the end of it, even though the whole time I was eating it, this old lady sitting under me kept glaring at me, giving me her version of the Bad Dog Look; that half-disgusted, half-reproachful look, perfected by my parents, which makes you feel as if you've just been caught dragging a lump of dog food onto the new white couch. I started to apologize, even though I hadn't dripped jam on her or anything, but then I thought, wait a minute, you're in New York City now, Sarah. You're wearing sunglasses. You're free. So I wiped my mouth and gave her my most charming Shelley smile until she looked away.

We were almost at my stop when I noticed this guy staring at me. "Excuse me," he said, moving closer. He was tall, with a lot of dark, curly hair and he had an accent. "Can you direct me please to Ninety-seventh Street and Riverside?" Never talk to strangers, particularly men, my father always warned. But this wasn't a man; this was a kid. Plus, he was carrying a cello. I play the cello. I wondered if I was giving off some kind of cellist vibes.

"I'm sorry," I said, hoping I didn't still have jam around my mouth. "I'm not from the city."

"I'm from Moscow," he said.

"Russia," I said, or something equally brilliant. I don't have a lot of experience with boys. Girls who play the cello and talk to bushes aren't in great demand in my high school. There was a kid at camp last year who liked me, Jason Fleck, but he was more comfortable with computers than with human beings and he never asked me out or anything.

The pause was getting awkward, so I offered him a muffin. He looked at the bag as if there were a bomb in it. But then he took one. "Thank you very much," he said.

"I think that one's cranberry nut," I said. And then it was my stop.

My heart was thumping as I walked up Broadway. I'd thought it was just greed that made me buy three muffins. Now it seemed like luck, or fate, or maybe even my weird prayers. I couldn't believe how brave I'd been, offering a muffin to a handsome stranger. I'd been in the city less than an hour and already I'd had an adventure. It was an omen; I knew it. Shelley would be so jealous. I wished I'd found out what his name was, so I could tell her—Sasha, or maybe Mischa.

I loved the way this neighborhood looked. I loved the stores. The street was wide, with lots of trees, and buildings with window boxes filled with flowers. I loved the look of the people, too: men with ponytails, mothers pushing strollers, everyone in shorts or jeans. This was a place where interesting people lived, not like the people I knew. I could fit in here really well.

I started hoping Mrs. Friedman was the kind of

person I could really talk to, more like a friend than an employer. Then I went off into this whole fantasy about her kids and how well we'd get along. As I walked past a school, I even imagined that when the summer ended, I'd be so indispensable they'd ask me to stay on and live in their spare room. My parents would protest, but would secretly be glad to get me off their hands. I had it all worked out.

Then I met Mrs. Friedman.

CHAPTER 2

Mrs. Friedman was not the kind of lady you picture someone calling Mom. She was built like a buffalo, and her voice was loud and ringing, like an actress or an opera singer, and she had these big, thick glasses which made her eyes look huge, the way a fishbowl can make goldfish look all looming and gigantic. She was wearing this long, loose top in a purple, green, and orange jungle print, and these matching leggings with green lace around the bottom. But people don't usually wear long, dangly earrings with pajamas, so I decided she was wearing clothes.

Her daughter was one of the most beautiful kids I'd ever seen. She had long, thin legs and pale, pale skin and thick, wavy hair and eyes too big and dark for her small face. I figured she was twelve.

"So." Mrs. Friedman lowered herself next to me on the squishy, flowered sofa and gave me a big smile. Her teeth looked very white against her bright red lipstick. "Tell me all about yourself." The daughter, Emily, found a spot over by the windows and began pulling dead leaves off a hanging plant. The living room had big windows and high ceilings and a fireplace and really nice furniture, but it was a total mess. Here was all this fancy art and plants and stuff, but the paint was sort of peeling off the ceiling and there was an exercise bike in the middle of the rug and stacks of newspapers in the fireplace and a messy desk with a computer and a huge piano piled with books and magazines.

"You're fifteen, isn't that right?"

I nodded. Mrs. Friedman's perfume smelled exactly like grape jelly.

"And what sign are you?" she asked.

I told her my birthday was October 9.

"Libra." She nodded to herself. "Yes. I do see a few Venusian attributes, particularly around the nostrils. Libra's a bit blander than I'd like, but on the other hand, it might be a relaxing change. We could use a little of that Libran composure. . . ."

"Excuse me," I said. "I hope this doesn't end the interview, but I'm not bland." Bland was several notches lower than adorable.

Mrs. Friedman looked at me more closely. "Well, actually," she said, "that's good news. I'm a Leo. I like to have my way, but I'm not big on wimps." She smiled at Emily. "Of course, Emily's a Cancer, so she never gives me any trouble. We're terribly close, Emily and I. She's really quite the perfect child." Emily went over to the exercise bike, and without looking at anyone, climbed on and began to pedal. "I never paid much attention to astrology," Mrs. Friedman said, "but you write about something long enough, you get to believe in it. And I find it a great help. If you're interested, I have lots of books."

"No thank you, Mrs. Friedman," I said. This woman was starting to seem seriously strange.

"Please," she said. "Don't call me Mrs. Friedman. Only my butcher and the doorman call me Mrs. Friedman. Call me Florence. Not Flo. I can't abide Flo." She looked like a Flo, though. An ice floe, or a lava flow. Maybe an overflow. "Now, please don't get the idea I'm some kind of nut, with this astrology," she said. "I mean, I am a nut," she gave me another of those big smiles, "but mainly, I'm a writer. A writer's business, as we all know, is studying human nature." I thought I heard Emily groan, but when I looked over, she was staring straight ahead and pedaling hard, so it must have been the bicycle wheels, which squeaked each time they went around.

"You're a writer?" I said. "Sometimes I think I might turn out to be a writer."

"Oh, yes. I'm working on a novel," Mrs. Friedman was still smiling, "which I hope to finish up this summer. Which is one reason I'm desperate for a mother's helper. I absolutely can't afford any more distractions in my life." I shot another glance at Emily, but couldn't catch her eye. "Of course, I also write for magazines, which is why the astrology." She reeled off a lot of articles she'd written. I can only remember two now, one about eating fiber, and one called "Consider a Wig."

Emily, meanwhile, was pedaling faster and faster, as if she thought she'd escape from the earth's gravity if she only pedaled hard enough. I told myself not to judge a book by its purple, green, and orange cover and to work harder at making Mrs. Friedman like me, but I was also thinking what I needed was a job where the people were more normal than me, not weirder. Then she said something about quizzes.

"Quizzes?" I said.

"Oh, I do lots of quizzes," Mrs. Friedman said. " 'Are You Really Ready to Lose Weight?' 'What Is Your Charisma Quotient?' That sort of thing."

"Oh, I love taking those," I said, which is true. Whenever I get my hair cut or go to the dentist, I always look for quizzes in the magazines. I'm sure they'll tell me something important about myself. But I didn't expect Mrs. Friedman to jump on it quite so enthusiastically.

"Let's assume," she said, fixing me with those eyes, "you're about to be dropped on a desert island. You can only bring along one item. Do you choose (a) your Swiss army knife, (b) a hair dryer, (c) the complete works of William Shakespeare, or (d) a fifty-pound chocolate bar?"

"Is this an example," I said, "or am I supposed to answer?"

"That's up to you," she said.

"Well, in that case, definitely the chocolate," I said. No reaction from Mrs. Friedman. It occurred to me too late that I should have said the knife, to show how practical I was. "Oh well," I said. "Guess I blew that one."

"Now." Mrs. Friedman ran her fingers through her hair and I got another blast of her perfume. "You've been incredibly busy—exams, homework, whatever— and you get one precious hour to do anything you want. Do you (a) call your best friend, (b) go for a brisk walk, (c) do your nails, (d) clean the bathroom, or (e) climb into bed with a good book?"

"Florence," Emily said, "why are you doing this?"

"Emily," Mrs. Friedman sighed, "you know I'm trying to find someone who'll be right for you." She looked back at me, all eager and hyped up again. "So which will it be?"

"That's not the greatest question for me," I said. I hadn't had a best friend since the fifth grade. And I read all the time, but I like reading under my rhododendron, not in bed. "I'm going to have to say (f) none of the above."

"That's not one of the choices," Mrs. Friedman said. "Though I must confess, none of those things appeal to me particularly, either. And you're right, you're definitely not bland." She leaned toward me confidentially. "Do you know, a few of the girls I've interviewed actually chose cleaning the bathroom? I'm hoping they just said it to impress me; I mean, I'd adore a clean bathroom but someone like that would drive me absolutely bats. By the way, that's what I'd take, the chocolate." She looked at her watch. "God, I'm impossible. Twenty-five past ten and already it feels like lunchtime. Can you cook?"

"I'm not, like, a gourmet cook," I said, afraid now she was going to give me a cooking quiz.

She gave this sort of strange laugh. "That's probably just as well. I have to lose some weight, and Emily . . ." She got up and began fiddling with some papers on the desk. "But moving right along. You and your best friend have tickets to a concert. A boy you've wanted to go out with all year calls and asks you out for the same night. Do you (a) tell your friend . . ."

"You know . . ." I said. This was really starting to bother me. "Not to be rude, but what exactly is it you need a mother's helper for? I mean, my mom's friend said you had two kids but it seems like Emily's your only child. . . ."

"My son's away."

"And she's a little old to . . ."

"You have to understand," Mrs. Friedman interrupted me again. "I need someone who can get Emily interested in doing things. She used to have so many interests. Dancing, sports . . ."

"I'm interested in things," Emily said. Her face was red from pedaling but her expression was still all vague and distant. I didn't get it. Practically the first thing Mrs. Friedman said was she couldn't stand wimps, and yet there's Emily, and she's like, Wimp Extraordinaire. "I'm interested in lots of things," Emily said again in that flat, exhausted voice. "And I don't need a baby-sitter."

"She wouldn't be a baby-sitter," Mrs. Friedman said. "She'd be a mother's helper."

"I don't need one of those, either."

"Well, I do." Mrs. Friedman still had that chipper

smile, but when she took her glasses off, her eyes, which had seemed so oversized, looked ordinary, strained, and tired. "Emily," she said, "we've been over this a hundred times." Emily got off the bike and flopped into an armchair and picked up a book and pretended to read. "Emily," Mrs. Friedman said. "We agreed on this, remember? The choice was yours. We could have done it Daddy's way, but we didn't think that was a good idea. Now, am I right?" She went over and put her hand on Emily's shoulder. Emily didn't say anything but I could see her stiffen and I had the sudden thought that she might not be a wimp at all. What she was, I had a feeling, was another artichoke, with lots of thorny layers.

Mrs. Friedman took her hand away but went on with her big sales pitch: "I really think Sarah might be good company for you. Don't you think you could have a good time with Sarah? I mean, of all the girls we've met . . ." When it became really clear Emily was not going to respond, she turned to me. "Emily's into this morbid thing, lately. She used to have a ton of friends, but now all she does is ride that damn exercycle or lie around reading books about young girls with dread diseases."

"It's not just young girls," Emily said.

"I read a lot, too," I said to Emily.

"Then she wonders why she has no appetite," Florence said. "What she needs is more activities, but now that school's over, and with me so busy. . . ."

Suddenly, Emily stood up. "You can't just buy someone to be my friend," she said in this choked voice, and ran out of the room. I heard a door slam down the hall.

Mrs. Friedman started to follow her, but the phone rang and she rushed to the desk to answer it. "No," she said, then, "No, you don't need to talk to her," then a few more *no*'s and *yes*'s, then, in this really strained voice, "She's okay, Elliott. Everything is fine. I tell you, it's under control now." There was a long pause, then, louder, "We're handling it, Elliott. You don't believe me?" Then she began shouting and carrying on, saying things like, "You're the one who needs a shrink, Elliott. Don't you dare blame me for problems you started. You're the only crazy one around here."

It was awful. I'm a very nosy person but this was too much even for me. I started moving toward the door, but before I'd even gotten to the foyer, Mrs. Friedman turned and saw me. There was something about her face, the way she was trying to yell at her husband and at the same time act to me like everything was fine, that I just couldn't leave, so I muttered something about looking for the bathroom. "End of the hall," she said, still trying to smile.

The door at the end of the hall was closed. I was

debating whether to knock or just open it when I heard gagging noises. Oh Lord, I thought, now Emily's so upset she's sick. "You okay in there?" I called, wishing even more that I had left. The toilet flushed and I heard water running. "Emily, you okay?" I said again.

The door opened. Emily looked briefly at me, then down the hall at Mrs. Friedman, who was coming toward us. "I'm fine, really," she said, giving me this fierce, imploring look. "You don't have to say anything to her."

"Well, that little unpleasantness is out of the way," Mrs. Friedman said. "That was Emily's father." As if I hadn't guessed. "He doesn't call that often. But now I see you girls are talking. I'm so pleased. Sarah, I hope that means you'll stay."

"You're offering me the job?" I said.

"You're exactly what we're looking for," she said. "I'll pay you very well. You'll have a lovely room, with plenty of freedom to go off and do your thing and not a lot of cleaning and we don't care if you can't cook."

"I don't know," I said. If I was looking for these people to improve my life, I'd come to the wrong place. "This job isn't what I thought." I felt mad at them for not being the family I was hoping for: a basic father, a mother who was like your basic mother only nicer, and two cute basic little kids. But I also felt upset and sad for both of them, and that made me even madder.

"It doesn't seem like Emily even wants a mother's helper."

Mrs. Friedman's eyes got goggly and gigantic. I couldn't tell if she was going to beg, or yell, or go back into her phony smiling thing. I don't think she knew either. So there we were, standing in this hall, totally tense, nobody looking at anybody, not saying anything. Then Emily said, "It's all right with me if she wants to stay."

CHAPTER 3

I wasn't going to take the job. But, at dinner that night, I sat looking at my mother's perfect makeup and my sister's perfect hair, and at my turkey burger and my Tater Tots. I saw the way they smiled and nodded as Shelley's boyfriend, Bart—who, you understand, is about as scintillating as an anchovy—recounted his day bagging groceries at Shoprite. It wasn't just that everyone seemed more interested in him than in letting me talk about Emily and Florence. It was how bland it all was, how totally and terminally bland. I thought about the Russian cellist, and the look in Emily's eyes when she said she wanted me to stay. "You know something," I said. "I want to give the Friedmans' job a try."

"I'm not so sure," my mother said. "You hear so

many horror stories. And you yourself keep telling us this lady's something of a flake."

But finally she agreed to talk to Florence, and after a long chat, they decided I'd go in on Saturday. I'd work Mondays through Fridays, and go home on weekends. "Well," my mother said when she got off the phone. "She thinks you're absolutely great. And she's paying you a lot. I just hope she doesn't think she's hiring a maid."

The less said about that week, the better. My parents acted as if I were going to the Amazon. They kept upping the number of times per week they wanted me to call. I hadn't even left yet and they were planning what we'd do my first day off. So I shouldn't have been surprised when they wouldn't let me take the train in by myself. "We'd like to check these people out," they said. "Is that unreasonable?"

And check they did. I still thought Florence looked like a dressed-up bison in her gauzy, flowered skirt and tons of turquoise jewelry and her fuzzy, buffalo-brown hair, but practically the first thing she said when we arrived was, "Sarah is a jewel. I advertised the job as mother's helper, but the absolute minute I met Sarah, I knew I had to redefine. Sarah is not the ordinary mother's helper. Sarah will be Emily's summer companion." So that pleased my parents. They also liked the neighborhood and the building. Emily didn't smile much and she hardly said anything, but she looked really pretty in an oversized white T-shirt and white shorts.

The apartment was even more enormous than I'd remembered, with all these halls and corridors and archways and funny chandeliers. Nine rooms, Florence told my parents. You could imagine fifty years ago, when there was a maid to live in the maid's room off the kitchen, and a butler to pull things up in the dumbwaiter, and lots of kids to fill up all those rooms. Most of the apartment was the same strange hodge-podge as the living room, that mix of fancy stuff and funkiness and just plain mess, but Emily's room was like a picture in a magazine. Except for the exercise bike, which had been moved in from the living room, it was totally pink and perfect, with these twin beds with ruffled, pink-flowered bedspreads, a bare desk, two big bookcases with all the books evenly lined up, a row of dolls, and more stuffed animals than I'd ever seen. "Adorable," my mother said. My favorite word. "And so neat!" I could just see her noting how there were no clothes thrown over the chair, no books open on the bed, no dirty socks hanging out of a pair of smelly sneakers.

We brought my stuff to a bedroom down the hall from Emily's. "My son David's room," Florence said, as my father put my suitcase on the bed.

"It's great," I said. It had big windows on two sides, so it was really bright.

"He's off working as a counselor. At a music camp." Florence mentioned the name of the camp, which meant nothing to any of us.

"Aha," my father said, or some such thing.

"He's an extremely talented musician," Florence said.

"His room is very neat," my mother said.

"Not normally," Florence said. "I had Emily pack his things in boxes so Sarah could think of this as her room for the summer. We want her to feel totally at home."

And then, after more compliments and politeness on all sides, which, mercifully didn't take too long, my parents said good-bye to Emily and Florence.

"Looks like you'll be very comfortable here," my father said, as I waited with them for the elevator. I nodded.

"They certainly seem well off," said my mother. "And Florence is crazy about you, which is a good beginning. But I don't know about Emily. She looks like she's been ill."

"She's fine," I said, as the elevator arrived. "And I'll be fine. Don't worry."

"Call and let us know how the first day goes," my mother said. The elevator operator wasn't the old geezer in a uniform who'd taken us up. It was a young guy in jeans and I saw him eyeing me as we got in. "And don't let her make you work too hard," my mother said. And then, we were at the lobby and, after a few more final speeches, my parents left.

"So, you working for 14A?" the elevator guy asked us as I got back in. He pulled the elevator door shut behind us and turned to face me. He had amazingly smooth, brown skin and round, dark eyes, and shiny black hair. "What're you, the baby-sitter?" He smiled.

My head had been buzzing all morning, but now the electrons, or whatever they are, started zinging around faster than the speed of light. "Companion," I said. My summer was beginning. He even had an accent. "I'm going to be Emily's companion." I couldn't tell how old he was. Maybe nineteen, maybe twenty-one. I looked at his jeans and cowboy boots and wondered why he wasn't in a uniform.

"Angel," he said.

"What?" I said. No man had ever called me anything before, unless you count, like, uncles or shoe salesmen.

"Angel," he said again. We were at my floor. He pulled back the heavy gate and then the door. "I'm, like, telling you my name."

Now, I was blushing. "Sarah," I said. And shook

his hand, which may or may not have been what you're supposed to do, but it made me feel more in command.

"Well, see you around, Sarah," he said. Then, as I started to get off, he added, "Good luck," giving me this smile I couldn't read. "If you ever need anyone to talk to, just ring the bell. I'm usually on nights."

Something about the way he said "good luck," I wanted to ask him what he meant, but by the time I'd got myself together, the elevator had clanked down to the lobby.

"Emily," Florence called, as soon as I came in the door. "Emily, where are you? Come out so we can help Sarah unpack."

"That's okay," I said, when Emily didn't answer. "There's not that much." I didn't mind having a few minutes by myself to give my brain a chance to settle down.

But Florence gave a tinkly laugh and turned her volume up to high. "Emily, sweetheart," she bellowed, "we need you." Emily came into the living room, looking less than thrilled. "We have to help Sarah get settled in."

"Why do you need me?" Emily said.

"To keep us company, silly." Florence laughed again and led us toward David's room. "We're trying to get to know each other, right?"

She'd emptied out a chest of drawers for me. I'd

brought all the summer clothes I owned, which was basically shorts, jeans, T-shirts, my bathing suit, and my denim jacket. I had brought my best sneakers and my best jeans, but nothing remotely Flo-like. I could see Emily scrutinizing everything, but I couldn't tell what she was thinking. Florence, meanwhile, was smoothing piles, refolding all the things that I'd crammed into the suitcase any which way. "Well," she said, as she put my now neatly folded purple T-shirt in the drawer, "it's nice to see somebody likes colors besides me. Maybe you can get Emily to agree to wear something besides white."

"White's nice," I said. I mean, what was I going to say? I tried to catch Emily's eye, but she was fiddling with a pile of tapes.

By now, everything was unpacked except my notebooks. I could have waited till I was alone, but I wanted Emily to know something about me, so I sort of fanned the notebooks out on David's desk and lined up my pencils and pens alongside. "Oho, this looks interesting," Florence said. "You did say you were a writer." I nodded. "Journals?" she said.

"I've been doing it since I was thirteen," I said. "I'm up to my third notebook." I would have left the first two home except I knew no matter where I hid them, Shelley would dig them out and read everything I'd said about her.

"I have a journal," Emily said. It was the first thing she'd said to me.

Florence looked at her. "I didn't know that."

Emily lined up all the edges of the tapes.

"What do you write about?" Florence asked.

Emily shrugged. "Just things."

"I'm surprised you never mentioned it," Florence said. "Me being a writer and all. And David, too." She turned to me. "My son's been winning writing contests since he was a little boy."

That stopped the conversation dead, until Florence decided I needed to learn to use all the appliances and electronic stuff. She showed me the answering machine and the fax and the computer. We proceeded to the kitchen, where she gave me a whole detailed demonstration with the cappuccino maker. I said I didn't drink coffee, but she said that was the only thing her husband ever did that she still missed, making her coffee in the morning. I saw a look flash across Emily's face when Florence said that—anger, sadness, I wasn't sure what it was—but for the instant it lasted, it was really strong. Then we stood there, nobody quite looking at anybody, until Florence suggested lunch. "We'll walk around and show Sarah the neighborhood," she said.

"Great," I said, thinking we'd all feel more comfortable outside the apartment. I brushed my hair and put

on lipstick, which I almost never do, but instead of
Angel, the eighty-year-old man in the blue uniform
was running the elevator. Florence called him Clifton.

"Who was that young guy who was here before?" I
asked when we got out.

"Who, the gorgeous one?" Florence's voice rang out
all over the marble lobby. "That's Angel." I prayed
the doormen were both deaf. "He's the super's son. He
is cute, isn't he? Emily thinks he's cute, too, don't you,
Em?" Emily was pretending she didn't know Florence.
"He's a smart boy and, wouldn't you know it, he's a
Leo, just like me. I gave him my charisma quiz the
other day and you wouldn't believe his score. Hello,
Hector, Eddie." Florence nodded to the doormen.

It had turned into a hot, muggy afternoon. The
trees in Central Park were limp and dusty and the
flowers in the window boxes looked ready to conk out
from the heat. As we walked to Columbus Avenue and
turned downtown, Florence pointed out the cash machine, the place where Emily had gone to nursery
school, and her fish market. It was hard for me to
concentrate. I was too busy trying to figure out everything that had happened.

We passed by lots of hamburger places, a few
trendy-looking bars, and a ton of Chinese restaurants,
but the only place Florence and Emily could agree on
was this funny health food store with tables in the

back, behind the bins of dried fruit and granola. The waitress had six earrings in one ear. I ordered the tuna melt and a large fresh grapefruit juice, which I drank in about two gulps. Florence got salade *nicoise*. "I'm being virtuous," she said. Emily ordered steamed vegetables and a bottle of mineral water. "Emily, for God's sake, order something besides vegetables," Florence said. "At least get some grain, some protein, something."

"You're not on a diet?" I said. Emily shrugged. "Why?" I said. "You're so beautiful."

"Don't ask," Florence said, as Emily picked out the bean sprouts. "Emily, here, do us both a favor." She held out her roll. "Have my bread."

"I don't want your bread," Emily said.

I ended up eating her bread and drinking another large grapefruit juice as well. Then Florence paid the check and we went home.

When we got back, Emily went right to her room and closed the door. I couldn't tell if Florence expected me to go in after Emily, but it was pretty clear Emily did not want company, so I followed Florence to the kitchen. "Is there something I should do?" I said. "Would you like some help with something?"

Florence pulled a bottle of diet Coke from the refrigerator and poured us each a glass. "Why don't you and I just relax and get to know each other," she said.

She handed me my glass, took her soda and the bottle, and I followed her to the living room. "I'm sure Emily will be out to join us in a minute," she said, settling into the flowered sofa.

Emily didn't come out till dinner, which we ordered from a Chinese restaurant, and then only because Florence made her. So Florence and I basically spent the rest of the day on that flowered sofa. Which was fine, I guess. I learned a lot about astrology, and all the articles Florence had written, and about Emily as a little girl. I told her about school and everyone in my family. I liked her. She was interesting, and she got my jokes, which is more than you can say for my family. And she was a good listener when you were alone with her, if you didn't mind that she kept interrupting to guess everybody's rising sign and ruling planets. It was actually a lot more comfortable being with her without Emily around. It was just that, here I was, in this terrific New York job, with no clue what anyone expected me to do.

I didn't say anything to my parents when I called. But that night, lying in David's empty room, listening to the roar of traffic on the street, watching the bands of yellowish light flicker on the ceiling, I kept thinking about how Angel wished me luck. And I found myself saying a small prayer: Please, let this job work out.

CHAPTER 4

Over the next few days, I tried every way I knew to make friends with Emily. I asked her about herself; I asked what she was reading; I tried to tell her about me. She was never mean or anything. She just treated me as if I were the doorstop or a potted palm. I could tell she was interested in me, because I'd catch her looking at me when she thought I wasn't watching. And more than once, her eyes flicked to mine when Florence said something totally outrageous. But when I suggested we go out for a walk, or rent roller skates in Central Park, or even go over to a video store and get a movie, she gave me that flat, distant look and told me she had things to do. Which meant either reading, or riding what even I was beginning to call "that damn exercycle."

I could have hung out in the living room with Florence, who was glued to the computer trying to make a deadline on some article about wrinkles. She called me in so often to bring her diet soda and ask how things were going, I knew she wanted me to keep her company. But it was too intense for me: books and papers strewn all over, the printer grinding pages out onto the floor, Florence glaring at the screen and talking to herself.

Instead, I lurked around feeling out of place, and stared out the window at all the cool-looking people I was never going to meet, and looked in the mirror. I always made fun of my sister for spending so much time looking in the mirror. "Yup, still the same old ugly Shelley who you saw the last time," I would say, or stuff like that. And here I was checking myself out constantly, making the rounds of every mirror in the house. I kept thinking I looked older. Better. Maybe even a little sexy. But then I kept having to go back and check to see if it was really true.

True or not, it did me no good whatsoever. We barely left the apartment. All week, I saw no males at all except the window washer and Mr. Farber, from the laundry room. It turned out Emily had a thing about being clean. She changed her clothes at least three times a day, which I didn't notice at first, since she always wore white running shorts and a white

T-shirt. And Florence may have been a total slob, but she was a fanatic about clean laundry. She said seeing a pile of dirty clothes made her feel out of control. I'd quickly learned you do not want to be anywhere near Florence when she feels out of control. It takes two forms—way too pleasant, as in, "Emily sweetheart, will you be an absolute love and run down and do a wash?" said smilingly, but with this sort of undercurrent, so that you know if you don't do it that instant, she'll detonate; or so tense you're terrified she'll attack you. But if you do what she wants, she'll tell you how wonderful you are and how she couldn't possibly survive without you. Emily, needless to say, did what Florence wanted. So Emily and I spent a lot of time in the laundry room, not talking, just watching the clothes go round and round.

The first few times we went down to the basement, I fixed myself all up, on the chance I might see Angel. Florence had told me he lived with his family in the superintendent's apartment. But the only person we ever saw was Mr. Farber, an extremely old man who did his wash in a suit and tie and who always called Emily "Toots."

Mr. Ringelheim, the window washer, was even older. The thought of him hanging out the window on that belt contraption, fourteen floors above the street, was totally alarming. While he was in the bathroom filling up his pail, Florence told me he liked to talk so much, one time he'd actually fallen out somebody's window. "It was only from the second floor, thank God," she said, "but he's never been the same."

"*Oy*, so grown up!" Mr. Ringelheim said, when he saw Emily. "I remember when you were just a chubby little girl. My little Chubby Cheeks. Remember how I always called you that?"

It was an obnoxious thing to say, but I was amazed at how upset it made Emily. "I hate that man," she said, before he'd even completely climbed out the kitchen window. "I hope he falls." She looked about to cry. I'd been there for five days by that time, so when she took off for her room, I followed her and knocked on the door. "Go away!" she said.

I told her it was me, not Florence. "Can I come in?" I said.

"Why?" she answered. "So you can pinch my chubby little cheeks?"

I opened the door. She was on the bike. "He's an old fart," I said. "He didn't mean anything. It's not like you have chubby cheeks." She was pedaling so hard I thought she'd hurt herself. "He's not talking about the way you are now," I said. "Plus, the way he squints, he probably can't even see you." I did an imitation of him, but she wasn't looking at me.

I kept going like that, telling her how thin her cheeks

were, trying really hard, but all it did was make Emily pedal harder and make me feel like a failure. So after a while I gave up and went back to my room and lay on my bed until Mr. Ringelheim came to wash my windows.

I was getting tired. Part of it was being cooped up in the apartment, not doing anything, but also, I wasn't sleeping well. There were all these noises on the street: people yelling in strange languages, ambulances, car alarms, fire engines, a car horn that played Beethoven each time the car backed up, some guy who seemed to think he was a rooster. I know this because the first few nights, I actually jumped out of bed and ran to the window every time I heard something.

"Try some hot milk," my mother suggested one of the times I called. "Hot milk is always soothing."

"I hate milk," I said. "How could you forget that?"

"Well, you'll be back in your own bed in a few days," she said. "Daddy will be waiting at the station Saturday. I've bought a nice roast beef. I know you don't hate that."

She could probably hear my stomach growling.

I'd been hungry the whole week. One thing about living with a kid who hardly eats is you feel like a total pig if you eat normally. I'd offered to help Florence with the cooking, but so far, she'd done it all herself. And so far, we'd had the same thing every night: a boiled chicken breast just sort of lying in the middle of the plate, plain rice, a pile of carrot sticks and some steamed broccoli and zucchini. Florence always scarfed hers down in twenty seconds flat, but Emily had to inspect it all and push it around the plate and practically cut up every rice grain with a knife. And we'd just sit there watching this, till Emily said, "I'm done," and Florence said, "That's not all you're going to eat?" and they'd repeat some variation of that a few times and then Florence would eat the rest of Emily's. The day the window washer came, Florence ate all of Emily's.

Thursday night, I sat up late with Florence watching a show about prairie dogs. It was so dull I was sure I'd go right to sleep, but no sooner was my light off and my pillow all arranged than these cats started howling in the alley. I knew it was cats but it sounded like people crying. They quit eventually, but then Rooster Man started cock-a-doodling. I got up and closed the windows, but it didn't help. Plus, now I was way too hot. I was also hungry. Lonely and hungry is a killer combination. I tried writing in my journal, but that only made me lonelier.

I held out until 12:42 A.M. Then I felt my way down the dark hallway and bumbled through the living room and dining room to the kitchen. It took some more fumbling around before I found the light. When I flipped it on, cockroaches skittered across the counters, racing for the drain. Which reminded me I hadn't called my mother for a few days. I'd thought about it, but I didn't want to call again till I had something good to say. Anyway, I stood there for a bit, sort of reconnoitering. Then, nervous but exhilarated, I closed the kitchen door. There is something definitely exciting about being alone in someone else's kitchen. It's one of the big pleasures of baby-sitting. Of course, I lived here now, so in theory, it wasn't someone else's kitchen, but even so, my heart was racing as I opened the refrigerator.

The refrigerator was a major disappointment. All I found, except for mustard and ketchup and that sort of thing, were the same carrots and boiled chicken we'd had for dinner.

I poured myself a glass of diet Sprite and ate three pickles and decided it was time to move on to the cabinets. It was a big old kitchen and there were lots of cabinets, so it took a while to find the goodies. For a lady on a diet, Florence had good stuff: in the far corner, way up on the top shelf, I saw three bags of Pepperidge Farm cookies, a box of Mallomars, pretzels, a huge bag of nacho-flavored corn chips, and a bag of mini-chocolate bars. The problem was, there was a sign taped across the whole front of the shelf. I couldn't believe it. She'd actually drawn a picture of a

Hershey bar with a slash through it, like a No Smoking sign, and written: Florence: Fortitude! Don't Do Anything You'll Regret Tomorrow!

I knew I should just go back to bed but then I thought, it's not reasonable to expect a fifteen-year-old girl to survive on boiled chicken breasts, so I pulled a chair over and climbed up. Florence hadn't taped the packages together, so I reached behind the sign and one by one, removed them. I used the technique I'd perfected while baby-sitting: you take one of this, a smidge of that, then sort of rearrange what's left so nobody can tell how much is gone.

I had a Mallomar in my mouth and a Mint Milano in my hand and was just starting to climb down with the bag of Brussels when I heard a noise. It was footsteps, and they were definitely coming toward the kitchen. I froze. I heard a light click on. I stuffed the Mint Milano cookie in my mouth. My mouth was so full now I could hardly chew. Florence was going to hit the roof. I mean, she kept saying I should make myself at home, but I'd seen how totally enraged she got when Emily did the slightest thing that wasn't Florence's idea. The kitchen door opened. Quickly, I choked down the whole dry, scratchy lump of cookie.

And turned to see not Florence, but Emily, in a long T-shirt and sweatpants, looking as startled and guilty as I'm sure I did.

CHAPTER 5

Emily pulled herself together before I did. "What are you doing up there?" she demanded.

I managed to get the wad of cookies safely down my throat and climbed off the chair. "*Whew!*" I said. "I was terrified you were Florence."

"It's a good thing I'm not." Her hands were on her hips and her mouth was so tight that you almost couldn't see her lips. "She wouldn't exactly like it, you sneaking in to steal her food."

I looked down at the bag of Brussels, which I was still holding. From force of habit, I'd gone immediately into Bad Dog Mode, a horrible and frequent state at home. But then I thought, wait a minute. What's *she* doing, creeping in here in the middle of the night? So

I said, "I'm not stealing. I'm starving. I'm really glad I found these cookies. How can anyone survive on thirteen rice grains and a carrot stick?"

"What are you talking about?"

"Just, it's pretty funny, when you think about it, both of us tiptoeing in here for, like, this secret midnight junk food raid."

Emily wasn't laughing. "That's not what I was doing," she said. "I was just taking a walk."

"Right. Me, too. Right to the kitchen." I held out the bag of Brussels. "Here. You must be even hungrier than I am. You didn't eat anything tonight. You missed another scrumptious—"

"I'm not hungry." Her voice rose. "I'm not hungry at all. And I don't eat junk food." She suddenly looked about to cry. "You don't believe me."

I brushed the crumbs off my nightgown. "Hey," I said. "I don't care if you eat some cookies. It's not like I'm going to tell. Obviously. Not that I really see why she'd care."

"Believe me, she'd care. She'd totally care. She can't stand it if you touch anything of hers without asking."

"Emily," I said, "she told me I should make myself at home. I think we should both relax and sit down and have some milk and cookies like two normal human beings, and have a nice time. I mean, as long as we're here. . . ."

"Milk's gross," Emily said. "And I told you, I don't eat junk food." But she unfolded her arms and sat down. "A lot of nights I'm not that tired," she said. "I don't sleep that much. So I come out and sit and sometimes I have a drink or something. Maybe I'll have a little diet Sprite."

"Have whatever you want," I said. I climbed up and got the other cookies down and put them on the table. "I really do have to compliment your mother on her taste in goodies." I sat down and took a Brussels from the bag. "She has all my favorites. What is with that weird sign, though?"

"My mother is so greedy," Emily said. "She has, like, no restraint whatsoever. When she gets going, she'll eat anything that can't run away. . . ." I laughed, which I immediately regretted, because Emily was dead serious. "Trust me," she said. "It's true. She admits it. That's why she looks the way she does. It made my dad totally disgusted, how obese she got."

"Well," I said, "I have this theory." I actually didn't have a theory till that instant, but I needed to say something. "About why I'll never get fat. My theory is, I think so much I burn up all the calories."

"That doesn't work," Emily said, her voice still tight with scorn. "One cookie has, like, seventy calories. Read the bag."

"It just has to be the right kind of thinking," I said.

"It has to be, like, really intense. It can't be, you know, I wonder if I should wear jeans or shorts today."

"I think constantly," Emily said. "I think all the time."

"And see, you're really thin."

"Right. Miss Chubby Cheeks."

"You're not still thinking about that?" I said. "Look at you. You look like a dancer, or a model." Which was true, even in her old T-shirt.

"You just can't see it," she said. "I'm fat."

"Well," I said. "All I know is I've been thinking really intensely all week. I'm going to have a few cookies."

"I'm telling you, she's going to know," Emily said. "She always knows."

"Aha!" I said. "So you have been known to eat them."

She didn't look at me. "A long time ago, when I was really fat."

"Don't worry," I said. "What we do, we each take one from the middle section of every bag, so it won't be so obvious. And if she does say something, we just tell her she ate them herself and she forgot." I got myself a glass of milk, which I never drink, but now that I'd brought it up, I was stuck. I poured Emily her diet Sprite. Then I raised my glass. "Why don't we have a toast?" I said. "How about, 'To Partners in

Crime?' " I waited for her to clink with me. "Okay," I said, when she didn't budge. "You think of the toast."

She picked up her glass. "*Salud*," she said, without much enthusiasm.

"Oh, come on," I said, "it has to be something more personal. Like, 'Here's to a great summer.' "

"My dad always says: '*Salud*.' "

"Fine. *Salud*." We clinked again. "What's the story with your dad, anyway? How come they got divorced?"

I thought I was just making conversation, so I wasn't ready when she said, "Me." What do you say to something like that? I told her it was dumb and that was not why parents got divorced. "It can be if the kid is bad enough," she said.

"What's bad about you?" I said. "Seems to me, you're about as unbad as they come."

"That's because you don't know me," she said. I pleated and unpleated the paper cookie cups for a while. Then, for lack of anything else to do, I took a swig of milk. I almost gagged. "*Eeooh*, gross!" I said.

"I told you," Emily said, as I wiped my tongue off with a napkin, then quickly chewed another cookie to get rid of the milky taste. "I told you it was gross. Okay. Here. I've got a toast." She raised her glass. "No more milk!"

"I'll drink to that," I said, raising my glass again. "Wait a minute. No I won't." I jumped up and poured the milk down the drain. "God, that was disgusting," I said. But I was sort of glad I'd drunk it, because nothing beats acting like an idiot to cheer up another person. She wasn't smiling but she was starting to loosen up a little bit. I rinsed the glass and poured myself some soda. "Well now," I said when I got back to the table. "What shall we sample next?"

"You haven't had one of the oatmeals yet," Emily said. She handed me the bag.

"Oh, oatmeal, *pooey*," I said. "What I want is chocolate."

She pushed the box of Mallomars across the table. "Have one of these then," she said.

"If you insist," I said. "But you have to have one too." I held one out to her. I could see she was dying for it, but she shook her head. "God, I'd forgotten how good these are," I said, as I bit into the squashy marshmallow. "You should really try it. One can't make you fat."

"You're not eating it right," she said. "You're supposed to take these tiny bites all around the edges, till there's no more rim. . . ."

"Then you sort of grate the chocolate off the marshmallow with your teeth," I said.

"How did you know?" she said.

"The Universal Art of Cookie Eating." I raised my glass. "To cookie eating." We clinked glasses again. "And to Florence, who made it all possible." I was starting to get giddy.

"What are you laughing about?" Emily said.

"Nothing," I said. "It's just, I had this weird thought. Do you think if you nuked one of these Mallomars it would explode?"

Emily giggled, which was a first. I'd hardly even seen her smile. "You better not try," she said.

"I'm not going to do it," I said. "I was just thinking it might taste really good. You know, like a toasted marshmallow, only chocolate, or like one of those S'mores things." I pulled another one out of the box. "I bet, actually, it would be great."

"You have to eat it, though," Emily said. It was amazing how good it made me feel to make her laugh.

"Really, you think I should do it?" I said. She made a silly face and shrugged. "How long should I do it for?"

"I don't know. Three minutes?" she said. We put the Mallomar on a plate and stuck it in the microwave and set the timer.

"Don't look in the window," Emily said. "You can hurt your eyes."

"I know, I know." I got myself another glass of

soda. "This is kind of fun, you know?" I said, as we waited at the counter.

"It's weird," Emily said.

"Well, I always say, in a serious situation, act serious. And in a ridiculous situation, by all means act ridiculous." By now we were both really giggly.

Emily stopped laughing. "Can you go to the store with me tomorrow? I think we should get new cookies."

"Definitely," I said, feeling this sudden surge of happiness. "I'll go. I'd love to do something with you. I'll go anywhere you want." Thinking finally, finally, she was starting to warm up to me. But the Mallomar was taking forever. "You know what I just thought of?" I said. "You're not by any chance a Girl Scout?" Emily shook her head. "I didn't think so. But you know what I wish we had right now? A Girl Scout cookie. A chocolate mint Girl Scout cookie. That would be really good in the microwave. Do they have Girl Scouts in the city?"

"Not in my school," Emily said. "I don't know if there are Girl Scouts in private school."

"Too bad," I said. "Girl Scout cookies are the best. I was a Girl Scout in the fifth grade for about fifteen minutes, but they didn't give you any cookies. It was just all this saluting and rules and stuff. I couldn't deal with it. My sister was a Girl Scout."

"Is your sister nice?" Emily said. That was another first. Till now, she'd never shown the slightest interest in my life.

"If you like the type," I said.

"What type is that?" she said.

"Adorable. And perfect."

"Sounds like my brother, the perfect part." She hesitated. "Are you going back there this weekend?"

"I guess," I said. I was not expecting that. "I mean, they think I am. I mean, that's what we arranged. . . . Why?"

"I don't know." Emily shrugged. "I'm just asking."

But before I could pursue this, the microwave went off with a gigantic ding. Emily clapped her hand over her mouth.

"Oh God!" I said.

"You woke up Florence," Emily said. "I know it. She's going to have a fit." We stood there, barely breathing, for what seemed forever, Emily looking panic-stricken, me feeling, once again, like a totally bad dog.

Florence never came, but it sure killed the mood. That and the fact that the poor Mallomar had bubbled up like lava and then glued itself to the plate, so that I had to use a knife to scrape it off. Emily stayed around long enough to make sure everything was back where it belonged, but I could feel her itching to get away—

from me and any evidence that this had ever happened.

I lay in bed for a long time worrying about her, wishing I could understand what all this was about, thinking that compared to them, my mother and I weren't as bad as I had thought. I lay there thinking about all this and listening to the squeak of the exercise bike wheels as they went round and round.

CHAPTER 6

The next day, Friday, I was up before seven, but I waited in my room till Emily's door opened. "Morning," I said, as if I'd just happened to step out.

I hoped she might say something about the night before, or smile, or give me some sign that we were friends, but she just muttered "Morning," and headed for the kitchen. Florence, who was having coffee, immediately began telling us this dream she'd had about falling madly in love with her accountant, which was both embarrassing and incredibly dull. It reassured me, however, that she knew nothing about the cookie fest. Then, somehow, she switched from Morty the accountant to the importance of breakfast and the next thing I knew, the two of them were fighting. I'd seen versions of this same fight all week, but I found today's especially hard to take.

It started with Emily saying she couldn't eat the toast. "It's perfectly good toast," Florence said. "What's wrong with it? I bought it for you."

"It's got thingies in it," Emily said. She held it up by one corner, like a dead mouse.

"Those are walnuts and raisins, sweetie," Florence said, as if Emily were a three-year-old. "They have protein and minerals, and, if you'll excuse the expression, extra calories, which you need for energy. And, they're delicious. You always loved nuts. And raisins. Eat it," she ordered. "I want you to eat it."

I could see Emily's whole face harden. "They're wet and squidgy!"

"Then pick them out and eat the bread," Florence yelled.

"I can't," Emily yelled back.

"You'd better eat it, Emily. I'm warning you."

"I can't. I'll eat it later. I'm too full." Now Emily was whining.

"I really have no time for this." Florence stood up. "I have an article to write. Are you going to eat the damn bread or not?"

Or course she's not going to eat it, I felt like screaming. I can see it. Why can't you see it? But instead I said, really calmly, considering, "You know, Florence,

I just remembered, Emily and I decided last night to go to a coffee shop for breakfast."

I thought I might have to give Emily a kick under the table, but I was amazed. She pulled herself together and said, "That's right, Florence, we did."

"When did you decide that?" Florence said.

My heart raced. "Last night," I said. I thought it sounded somewhat lame, but Emily backed me up.

"Will you eat something there?" Florence said.

Emily nodded again.

"What?" Florence asked.

"I don't know," Emily said, not looking at her. "Something. Maybe some eggs. Something good for me."

Florence's eyes all of a sudden seemed huge and menacing behind her glasses. "I don't need to remind you, do I, Emily, about what your father said?" She said it very slowly. Emily shook her head. "Because we can do it our way, or we can do it his way. We don't want that to happen, do we, sweetheart?"

Emily shook her head again and in a small voice, said, "No."

Then Florence got her purse and handed me twenty dollars and squashed me in a perfumey hug. "Oh, thank you Sarah," she whispered. "I know I can count on you."

"We are not going to a coffee shop," Emily said the instant we were out the door.

"I know that," I said. "I'm not a complete dummy. We're going out to buy more cookies, in case she checks the bags. We're also going for a walk." I was feeling like I could easily walk twenty miles.

"I was sort of thinking we'd forget about the cookies," she said, as we rode down in the elevator.

"Yeah, but then she'll know," I said.

"You heard her saying I need calories. So maybe we'll just tell her that I ate them."

"Fine," I said. I wished I knew what Florence meant with her threats about Emily's father. But I had no chance to ask, because there was Angel, coming across the lobby. I grabbed Emily's arm. "Slow down," I whispered.

He caught up with us just as we reached the door. "You ladies are looking pretty cute today," he said, falling into step beside us. "Sarah, right?" I nodded, my heart boinging in my chest. "I never saw you again after that one time." He smiled at Emily. "I thought maybe she got fired."

"Uh-uh," I said. Not the world's most brilliant answer, but I'd evidently used up all my cool at breakfast.

"So which way you walking?"

"I don't know," I said. "Just walking."

"I'll walk with you as far as Eightieth," he said. The way he talked, "with you" sounded like "whichoo."

We started down the street, Angel on one side of me, Emily on the other. He wasn't as tall as I remembered. It was a nice day. "It's so great being out," I said. "You know, I've been in New York a whole week and I haven't been anywhere yet. I haven't seen a thing."

"Where you from?" he asked. When I told him, he said, "So you must of been to like, the Empire State Building or the Statue of Liberty?" I shook my head. "How 'bout the zoo?"

"Nowhere," I said, which wasn't strictly true, but I'd gone to all those places with my parents, so it didn't count.

"You need a tour, then," he said. "Definitely. A guided tour. What do you think, Emmy? Think we need to show Sarah the Big Apple?"

"I don't know," Emily said. She was dragging along as if she were upset. I, on the other hand, was starting to feel great. I mean, how could I not, with Angel looking at me as if my dumb remarks were the most original things he'd ever heard. And he was the best-looking guy I'd ever seen. I particularly liked his accent, which made, for instance, "exactly" sound like "essactly." Unfortunately, we got to Eightieth Street before I'd thought up something memorable to say. But before he left, he gave me another of those terrific smiles and said, "I'm serious. I'll show you around sometime."

"So now I suppose you're going to go out with him," Emily remarked after he'd turned the corner. It was pretty obvious she didn't like the idea.

"How should I know?" I said, hoping I wasn't blushing.

"You like him, right?"

"He's okay."

"Okay?" Emily said. "I saw the way you looked at him." She did a humiliating imitation of doggy adoration.

"You're crazy," I said. No question, now. I was blushing. "Anyway, he didn't say *me*, he said *us*. He'll show *us* around."

"Not us," Emily corrected. "You. I'm the little creep everyone wishes would go away."

"Emily!" I said, vowing to devote myself completely to her for the whole rest of the walk. "So what's the story with him," I asked, after we'd gone a few more blocks. "Is he, like, a career elevator man?"

"I don't know. I think he goes to college," Emily said. "Or wants to. Something." We walked some more. Then she said, "So do you have a lot of dates?"

"Yeah, right," I said.

"You don't?" she said.

"You don't have to rub it in," I said.

"No, it's just—I mean, if I were a boy, I know I'd want to go out with you."

"You would?" I said, making a stupid face to cover up that I was pleased. Then I said, "Listen, if he does ask me to do something with him, will you come?"

"You'd want me to come?"

"Why not?" I said, even though I wasn't totally sure that it was true.

Then we reached this shop that smelled like bubble bath, even from the street. "Come on," I said. "Let's look around." There were soaps the color of jewels, soaps shaped like fish and hearts and seashells, and shelves and shelves of oils and lotions and perfumes. We were the only customers in the store. I sprayed my wrist with something called Lavender Rain. "Think this'll help my sex appeal?" I said.

"I don't think you're supposed to just try them like that," she said.

"Then what do they have these testers for? Here. Sun on Water. Hold out your arm."

"I don't need perfume to make me stink," she said.

"Would you give it a rest," I said. I sprayed my other wrist. "*Ick*. Room deodorizer."

She picked up another tester and put her nose to it.

"Oh, here's one that's perfect for me. It smells like skunk."

"Emily, would you stop putting yourself down," I said. I picked up a booklet about how smells can change your mood. "I think you need aromatherapy," I said, spraying her with Strawberry Splash.

"Stop it!" she said. But she picked up another bottle. "I found the perfect one for you. Vanilla. You'll smell like a cookie."

"Here's Blueberry." I gave her a spritz. "You'll smell like a pancake."

"Or, wait," Emily said. "Here's a good one. Black Narcissus. Perfect for corpses."

I took a whiff. "*Eeooh*," I said. "It smells exactly like my Latin teacher, Mrs. Bushler." She giggled. I sniffed Evening in the Orient. "You think that corpse one's bad . . ." I grabbed my throat and made a gagging face.

Suddenly this tall, skinny salesman was looming over us. "May I help you ladies?" he said in this deep, snooty voice.

I was laughing so hard I could barely squeak out a "We're just looking," but Emily pulled herself up to her full height and fixed him with a Florence-like stare. "Yes," she said. She sounded like Florence, too. "It just so happens we're looking for a birthday present for my mother, but nothing here smells any good."

"I'm sure we can find something she would like," the salesman said. "How much did you want to spend?" I poked her in the back, but, without hesitating, she said, "Twenty dollars."

"We have some exquisite soap baskets," he said. And they were really pretty, all these gorgeous-colored soaps nestled in baskets shaped like seashells. But I practically fell over when Emily pointed to the biggest one and said, "We'll take that one."

I whispered, "That's Florence's money," but she reached in her pocket and took out a wallet. Then, as he led us over to the counter, she reached for a soap-on-a-rope and said, in that same haughty voice, "I'll take that too. Gift wrapped, please."

As soon as we got outside, I cracked up again. "You were great," I said. "I couldn't believe it."

"I hated the way he was looking at you," she said.

"But buying out the place? Isn't that going a little far?"

She shrugged. "I wasn't lying. It is my mother's birthday in a few weeks. I have to get her something."

"I love your Queen Florence voice," I said. "I have either totally underestimated you or that aromatherapy's great stuff."

She suddenly reached in the bag and held out the gift-wrapped soap-on-a-rope. "I got this for you," she said.

Needless to say, I was surprised, especially since I'd thought it was a man's gift, but I thanked her over and over. "This was such a good idea, going out," I said. "We should do this all the time."

"Okay," she said.

Which made me say, "Remember last night? When you asked me was I going home tomorrow?" She nodded. "It's not like I miss them or anything. I don't have to go."

"Are you sure that would be all right?" she said. We kept on walking downtown, but Emily was getting all tense again. "We've got to go to that coffee shop," she said. So we walked over to some place on Broadway, one of those diners with the revolving shelves filled with strawberry-studded, whipped-cream loaded, chocolate-curl sprinkled chocolate cakes twelve inches high. Which is, of course, what I ordered. I mean, I'd been on Florence rations for a week. Emily ordered juice, poached eggs on an English muffin, and a side of toast.

I gave the cake my full attention the instant the waitress set it down, so it took me a while to notice that Emily was sitting there holding her fork and shaking her head. "I can't eat this," she said, her eyes filling with tears. "It's too disgusting. It's making me gag, just looking at it."

The waitress walked by carrying two cups of coffee,

then came back. "Somethin' the matter, honey?" She had goldfish-colored hair and one of those raspy New York voices. "Eggs too loose?" Emily looked ill. "I'll send 'em back, firm 'em up a little, if you want."

"No," Emily said. "Just take them away. Please."

"How 'bout the toast?" the waitress said. "Gonna eat the toast?"

"It's got all that butter running down it," Emily said. And when the waitress left, *tsk-tsking* about kids today, Emily said, "I tried. You saw me, Sarah, right? I really tried."

"Want some of my cake?" I said.

"No!"

"Don't cry." I have a real problem when people cry, even if it's just some character on television. I get this stinging in my nose and I feel totally unhinged. "It's okay," I said. "It's all right with me if you don't eat it. I'm not your mother."

"You don't understand," she said. "You don't understand anything. I have to eat. They're going to do something terrible to me if I don't."

CHAPTER 7

"They put you in a hospital and stick tubes down your nose," Emily said. "That's what my father told me. He said they strap you to a bed and feed you through your nose until you're fat."

"No one's going to do that," I told her. "It's revolting. Plus, it's crazy. He's just trying to scare you."

"That's what he said," Emily insisted. "I swear. He wants to fatten me up. Like a pig. Like a turkey, for Thanksgiving. Like a big fat blimp." We were still sitting in the coffee shop. The waitress had long ago removed my empty plate and though Emily had stopped crying, she looked like she could start again at any minute. Either that or explode. "He hates my mother for being fat and then he wants me to be just like her. He said if I don't start eating, he'll put me in a mental hospital where they tie you up until you eat."

"Come on," I said. "That's like something from the Middle Ages. Your mother'd never let him do that. I mean, Florence is tough. This is Queen Flo we're talking about, here, not some little wimp."

"Yeah, well, he's a lawyer," Emily said.

She fiddled with the salt shaker, turning it round and round. I found myself staring at her fingers. I am, despite my other strangeness, a normal-sized person, and my fingers were veritable salamis next to hers. Not to mention her wrist, which looked like you could snap it as easily as a twig. You have to be really thin for your fingers to lose weight.

How could I not have noticed this, I thought suddenly. How could I not have seen? Part of it was the baggy T-shirts, and part of it was, she was so pretty it was hard to see that anything was wrong, but it shook me up, seeing for the first time how spindly she was. "She's not going to send you away," I said again, this time mostly to reassure myself.

"She said she wouldn't." Emily still didn't look at me and she spoke so softly I could barely hear. "That's why she got you."

"What?" It might have been the cake, but I suddenly had this dull lump taking up all the space between my stomach and my throat.

"She didn't tell you that, but I heard her on the phone with my father. And you heard her today. 'I'm counting on you, Sarah.' That's what she said, right?"

"What am I supposed to be doing?" I said. "I don't know anything about this. Nobody said a word about me making you eat."

"I eat," Emily said. "I eat what my body needs. I just don't stuff myself like a disgusting pig, that's all. That's what none of you understand."

"Everything okay here?" The waitress paused at our table.

"What do you care what I eat?" Emily said. "Why is that all anyone thinks about? Food, food, food! It makes me sick!" And she got up to leave.

"Where are you going?" I said.

"To the bathroom," Emily said. "I have to go to the bathroom. Is that all right with you?"

The waitress shook her head as Emily headed for the back. "You got problems," she said. The offhand way she said it really made me mad, but then I thought I saw a flash of kindness in her eyes and wished that I could ask her what to do.

"Couldn't they just send you to a shrink?" I said, when Emily got back, before she'd even had a chance to sit. "I know plenty of people who go to therapists. Lots of kids in my school, for one, not to mention this person from camp, Jason Fleck, who I briefly considered as a boyfriend and whose parents were going through a terrible divorce. Divorces can be rough. And Jason really loved his therapist." Emily gave me what is generally called a withering look. "I'm not saying you're crazy," I said. "Jason wasn't crazy. Extremely peculiar, yes . . ." I knew I was babbling but I couldn't stop. "You don't have to be crazy at all. . . . It's just, what I'm trying to say . . . I don't know if I'm the exact right person . . . I don't know anything. . . ."

"I went," Emily said. "It did me no good whatsoever. The lady was so dumb. All she did was ask me stupid questions. Plus, she was so fat herself. She was jealous of me because I can control myself."

"So you stopped going?"

"Even Florence said it was a waste. So then Elliott wanted me to go to this mental camp somewhere, where he said they'd help me with my quote, problem. But I said no way. And Florence didn't really want me with a bunch of sickies, either—that's what she called it, sickies—so I refused. So then . . ."

"Enter Sarah," I finished for her. She nodded. "Great. And now I'm supposed to save you," I continued. "How am I supposed to do that?"

"I don't need saving," Emily said, going back into her Queen Florence voice, which, after all this, I must say, sort of pissed me off.

"And here I thought I was just supposed to keep you company," I said. "Do a little laundry, clean the house, and keep you entertained. . . . I mean, I figured you were just this spoiled, rich kid who had no friends." Then, of course, I felt terrible and had to go into a whole long bumbling thing about how I didn't mean it and only said it because I was upset, and how I used to feel that way but didn't anymore. But then I gave it up and said, "So what did Florence tell your father?"

Emily took a deep breath. "That maybe if I was around someone more normal . . ."

I laughed. Or snorted. "Did she say that before or after she met me?"

"She really likes you. She keeps telling me. You're great with her."

"Right. Me, that noted genius with mothers. You met my mother. I'm death with mothers. Not to mention fathers and sisters."

"I liked your mother," Emily said.

"You only got a tiny glimpse," I said. "You should see us at home. It's like . . ."

Emily sat up straighter. "You fight a lot?"

I thought about that for a minute. "Fight's not exactly the right word. It's more like chronic, mutual getting on the nerves."

"So what do you do?" She was definitely starting to perk up a little.

"Spend a lot of time in my room . . . talk to my-self . . . commune with bushes . . . plot revenge. Sick, right? See, we're all sickies, in our own sick little way."

"But you're going home tomorrow, right?"

Something about the way she looked at me made me say, "I think I won't."

"It's your day off," she said.

"I told you I would stay," I said. "I'll call home as soon as we get back."

"Get you girls anything?" My old pal, the waitress, was hovering over us again. I saw that the coffee shop was filling up. The way Emily looked at her, for a brief minute I actually thought she might order some-thing. Which would prove Florence was right, that I was exactly what she needed.

It would have been nice, but it didn't happen.

"Just the check, please," I said, wondering what was really going on with Emily, and how on earth I was supposed to make it better.

CHAPTER 8

There were seventy-one books on anorexia in the New York Public Library. That's where I went on Saturday to find something that could tell me what to do. While Florence and Emily went off clothes shopping, and my family languished without my company (actually, they were quite calm about it), I sat in this huge room that was way too cold and smelled like school and plowed through all the books and magazines and journals.

I was really scared. I'd heard about anorexia for years, read the *People* magazine stories about teenage actresses who starve themselves, seen the "Movies of the Week." But it's totally different when you know someone who has it. And she did seem to have it. She was not as bad as most of the girls they talked about, but Emily was definitely anorexic, even if she did seem to be in the beginning stages. And every book I read said anorexia tended to get worse, that treating it was really hard and didn't always work. And they all kept talking about girls who didn't want to change.

Part of me wanted to run out of there and take the next train home. But I kept thinking about what she told me in the coffee shop and forced myself to keep on reading.

There was this guy across the table from me. Every time I looked up, he was staring at me, licking his mustache. Picture one of those *National Geographic* specials on sea lions in mating season and you'll know exactly what he looked like. I'd been trying to ignore him. Then I tried crossing my eyes and giving him ferocious looks. But he evidently thought that meant I thought he was cute, so finally I said, "Buzz off! You can see I'm working. Go leer at someone else!" He looked hurt, but he did take his books and move. That was fairly satisfying, but by then I'd been there for four hours and my brain was numb and I still had no answers, so I gave it up and headed back to the apartment.

I had to talk to Florence. That was obvious. How to do it was the question. I spent the whole bus ride thinking up ways to ease anorexia into the conversation. But when I walked in the door and Florence said,

"Hi, there!" smiling brightly, as if everything was peachy keen, I couldn't bear it.

"I went to the library," I said. "That's where I've been all day. Reading about girls like Emily."

"Girls like Emily?" Her mouth was still smiling but her eyes darkened. "I don't think I follow."

She was looking really large to me all of a sudden, but I kept going. "It's hard not to notice, Florence. Emily's got an eating problem. I know we've all been acting like . . . you know, sort of pretending."

"Pretending? When have I pretended anything? Name me one instance." She started toward the bedrooms. "Emily!" she yelled. "Are you on that damn bike again? Get off it and come in here. Sarah's back."

"No, please. Wait a minute." I felt scared to see Emily, afraid she'd be even skinnier than I remembered. I wished desperately there were someone here to help me. But I also knew I had to say it. "Florence, she has anorexia."

"Oh. This is supposed to be big news?" she said. "You think you're telling me something I don't know? Just because I don't care to use some trendy TV talk show label. . . . Give me a break, Sarah. I live with it. You see me trying to deal with it. I'm knocking myself out here, dealing with it." She was shouting now.

I said it anyway. "She needs help, Florence."

"You've been here exactly one week, Sarah, and I

don't appreciate what you're implying. . . . You
hardly know Emily. You certainly don't know me."

"I'm sorry," I said. "But I went to the library. I've
just read all these books and articles. . . ."

"And now you're an expert on anorexia. You think
I haven't read the books? I've read dozens of books.
Hundreds of them."

Then Emily was in the doorway. "What's going
on?" she said. "Why are you shouting?" She looked
upset, but that's not why I was gaping at her. I was
gaping at her hair. Her beautiful long, wavy hair suddenly had spiky bangs. And layers. Plus, the whole
front was sprayed up into this stiff sort of crest.

"What happened to your hair?" I blurted out. Not
the right thing at all.

"I told you Sarah would hate it," Emily said. "I told
you that. I look hideous. I look like a stupid jerk."

"It's nice," Florence said. "I think it's nice." She
turned to me. "She's just upset because I told Robert,
he's my stylist, to do something a little more teenage."

Her hair made me remember, suddenly, a girl on
my sister's cheerleading squad who wore her hair
that way, who'd stopped eating and had to go to the
hospital.

"Sweetie pie, I only had him do it to cheer you
up," Florence said. "Besides, knowing you and all the

showers you take, you'll wash the whole style out by dinnertime."

Emily didn't say a word, just stood there not looking at me, twisting the cord from the venetian blinds around her finger.

"Fine, so everyone's mad at me," Florence said. "Now what?"

"Florence, I'm not mad," I said. "I'm just trying to talk to you guys about—"

"You've both gotten me so upset that I almost forgot to tell Sarah our news," she said. "We have good news. Right, Emily?" Emily ignored her.

"I'm sorry, Emily," I said. Emily ignored me.

"We're having a party." Florence talked right over me. "Which goes back to what you and I were just discussing, Sarah. Things I'm doing. It's my birthday on the twenty-eighth." She rolled her eyes. "Do not ask how old I am. I'm approaching hag-hood. But be that as it may, I thought I'd throw myself a giant bash."

"What does that have to do with Emily's problem?" I said. Once again, Sarah and her light touch. But this time, I avoided the dreaded word and this time Florence was ready for me.

"It has to do with how depressed we've been. We both need something to take our minds off things, a

project, something to celebrate. A party's a perfect
project. It's a great idea. And this party is going to be
fabulous. I even know what we're going to wear." She
described some dresses they'd just seen in Bloom-
ingdale's. "We have three weeks and a lot to do. I'm
inviting every eligible man I've ever met. Oh, and I
was thinking, Emily," she added, super casually, "we
should invite some kids for you."

Emily dropped the cord. "Florence, you . . ."

"She has a lot of friends at school, you know."

"I do not," Emily said.

"Well, you certainly used to. And they'd come if
you invited them. It would be good for you to be with
other girls. It's too bad you're not a Leo, like me,
sweetheart. We Leos are famous party animals. We
thrive on stimulation and excitement. Speaking of
which . . . ," she walked over to her desk and picked
up an address book, "I'd better get on the phone and
see who's going to be in town that weekend."

So the party animal made phone calls and Emily
stalked off to her room and it was pretty clear to me
that I had been no help. Florence talked some more
about the party during dinner. I didn't hear a word she
said. I was too busy watching Emily cut a stalk of
broccoli into tiny cubes and spear them one by one.

About ten o'clock, I called my parents. The phone

rang six times and then I heard my dad: "Please leave your name and number and the time of your call and any brief message. Remember, you must wait for the beep." I always hated that pompous message. I waited for the beep; then I hung up without saying anything. What was I going to say? Beep! Emily's got anorexia. Beep! They expect me to do something about it. Beep! Get me out of here!

Then I went into Emily's room. I'd never done that, just walked in on Emily when she had the door closed. She was lying there with her eyes shut and all the lights on. It was stifling but she had the covers up around her neck. She was hugging an old brown teddy bear and tucked around her was her whole collection of stuffed animals, at least twenty of them.

"Emily, are you awake?" I whispered.

"No," she said. "Leave me alone."

"Listen," I said. I had this speech I'd been practicing all night, that started, "Listen Emily, if you can think of any ways that I can help you with this eating thing . . . ," but something about those moth-eaten, matted animals—I got this stab of loneliness so sharp that for an instant I could hardly breathe. "Emily," I said, "I'm sorry about your hair. I was just so shocked she did that to you." She stirred as though she was going to say something, but she didn't. "I don't care if your hair looks stupid," I said. "You can have stupid hair. You can be fat or skinny or anything and I won't care. You're my friend, Emily. We're friends."

She clutched the teddy bear closer, and I thought I heard a little noise—a sigh, or it might have been a sob. Then she turned toward the wall.

"But Emily," I said, "I'm worried about you. Don't get any skinnier, Emily. Please."

CHAPTER 9

I must have gotten through to her. Or maybe, she and Florence had a talk. Anyway, something changed, because Emily started eating. She was spending just as much time on the exercise bike, and for lunch she still ate only a few bites of cottage cheese and cantaloupe, but she was eating dinner. I could hardly believe it. Beginning the next night, she started eating a little meat—"the butcher promised me it has no fat at all," Florence insisted, "and if I see one more chicken breast I swear I'm going to break out clucking"—all her vegetables, the occasional roll, and once, a baked potato, without butter. You can't imagine how relieved I was.

And, much as I hated to admit it, Florence was right about the party project. It was better being busy. Florence had this gift for getting you totally involved in things you didn't care about at all. Like the invitations: how many people to invite and would anyone come or would they all be out of town? And should she do poached salmon or Tex-Mex, and what kinds of hors d'oeuvres, and how on earth would she find a decent caterer on such short notice? Plus, she insisted on weighing all her food so she could lose five pounds and buy the dress. Plus, the apartment, as we all know, was a disaster.

She got Emily to fax all the invitations and make the lists. Emily liked organizing anything, so that was fine. I became Chief Cleaner. Which was also fine. It was a relief to have some project I could finish and say "Ooh, hey, look what I did." Plus, every time I finished something, Florence laid the praise on with a trowel. My family has always had more of an eye-dropper approach, so all it took was a couple of those gushy compliments and I was ready to take on the entire house. That's exaggerating, but that week, I did a lot of cleaning.

Sometimes, when Emily wasn't in her room riding the exercise bike, she cleaned alongside me, wearing rubber gloves and then taking a shower as soon as she was done. Florence was working on a quiz called How Do You *Really* Feel About Your Hair, so I made up some quizzes of my own, dumb stuff like, How Do

You Really Feel About Your Fur? What Kind of Party Animal Are You? Are You Secretly a Party Vegetable? Hearing me make jokes about her mother made Emily a little nervous, but we also laughed more than we had the whole time I'd been there.

We also went with Florence to every food shop and fancy market in the area, researching quiches, patés, chicken wings, and minipizzas. Emily loved going to the stores and picking the things out. She particularly loved going to the bakery sections, but she wouldn't try anything. She did, however, make a Party Possibles chart of everything we bought. She posted it on the refrigerator so we could rate the items on a scale of one to ten, ten being The Best Thing I Ever Ate and one being School Lunchroom.

So it turned into a good week for me. I told my parents that when they called. I didn't tell them anything of what was going on. I knew if I told them, they'd jump all over it and who knows what would happen then. So I kept it general, stuff like how this job was teaching me to deal with problems and that I was learning how to get along with different people. That I was working hard, but that I felt like I was being really helpful. And that they shouldn't be surprised if I stayed in New York City most weekends. I was testing out my independence, was the way I put it. "I hear you," my father said.

Thursday or Friday, Emily and I were in the dining room. I was standing on the table, trying to scrub ten years of greasy crud off the ceiling fan, and Emily was in the chair beside me, reading. Florence couldn't stand it when she read this book, which was a history of executions and plagues and disgusting practices through the ages, but Florence was out shopping. "What chapter are you reading now?" I said.

" '*Last Agonies of Historic Figures*,' " she said. "Listen to this. 'Alas! After an ill-fated night, His Serene Majesty's strength seemed exhausted to such a degree that the whole assembly of physicians lost hope and became despondent.' "

"You sound like you know that by heart," I said.

"I do. It's one of my favorites. King Charles. They drained out all his blood, practically, trying to cure him."

"Did it work?" I said.

"I guess not," she said. "He died. Would you like to hear '*Leeches and Bloodletting*'? It's my other favorite."

"Oh, great," I said. "The perfect accompaniment to scraping congealed flies off the fan." But I let her read it and I learned, among other nauseating facts, that all leeches have thirty-four body segments and can grow to eight inches long, and that Louis XIII of France was bled forty-seven times. It was a little gross for my taste, but one reason I didn't stop her was I could just hear Florence saying, "Emily, sweetheart, isn't there some nice cheerful book you could read instead?" and then, when that didn't work, screaming, "For God's sake, Emily, no wonder you can't eat!" Also in a bizarre way, it felt like Emily was giving me a gift.

"So how come you love this book so much?" I said after she'd read me this long drawn-out story about the poet, Keats, dying of tuberculosis.

She shrugged. "I just like reading it," she said. "It makes me feel better."

"Speaking of better," I said, "your hair looks okay now. The headband really works. It's fine now, don't you think?" I imitated Florence, goggling through her glasses: "I mean, tell me, sweetheart, how do you *really* feel about your hair?"

To which she said, "You do know she hired Angel?"

"*Huh?*" I said, still thinking about her hair.

"She hired Angel for the party. To help out. Serve drinks, whatever."

I almost dropped my Tuffy pad. "She didn't tell me."

"It was my idea," Emily said. And I knew that was another gift.

So the week passed. Sunday, Emily was in her room, exercising, and I was trying to clean the grubby little bathroom next to the kitchen, when I heard Florence talking on the telephone. This was nothing new;

she was on the phone constantly, but this time, her voice had that overly hearty ring that told me it was Emily's father. It was the same tone I'd used talking to my parents. I put down my spray bottle of scum remover. "Fine," I heard her say. "Things are really fine. No. We're getting along fine, we really are. I'm telling you, I'm very optimistic." I listened for my name. "This party idea of mine is working brilliantly. I'm not one to toot my own horn, but this time, I have to say, I really do deserve a toot. She's actually been eating a reasonable dinner this whole week." She enumerated what Emily ate. "Yes, without a fight. I think she may have even gained." There was another pause. I heard the refrigerator door close, then: "I don't know exactly. No, I haven't weighed her. You know she's very secretive about that. I don't like to push her. But I can tell by looking at her." Another long silence. "She hasn't lost any more, I guarantee you. Her attitude's much better. Having Sarah here's made all the difference." Her voice hardened. "No, it's better if you don't come. You'll just get her all riled up again." Then, "Soon, Elliott. I'm going to. I promise. I'll take care of it." The last thing I heard her say was, "I wish you'd trust me a little more, Elliott. I'm her mother. I have eyes. I'm with her all day long. I can tell when things are going better."

CHAPTER 10

I really did think things were going better. So I was shocked, the next day, when Florence took away the exercise bike. She didn't just take it out of Emily's room or put it in a closet. She actually called Arnold, the super, to lock it in the bike room in the basement. I was making my bed when the doorbell rang. I ran out when I heard Emily scream.

"What are you doing?" she cried, as the super dragged the exercycle toward the door. "You can't take my bike." The minute Florence closed the door, Emily began to shake. Literally quiver. "You can't do this," she cried. "I need it. How am I going to exercise?"

"I should have done this months ago," Florence said.

"Why?" Emily said. "What's wrong with it? I need

to exercise. What do you want from me? I'm eating. You wanted me to eat and I'm eating. . . . If I don't exercise . . ."

"It's wonderful you're eating. Now, if you don't exercise ten hours a day I can worry a little less about you losing weight."

"I'm not doing it to lose weight," Emily said. "I haven't lost any more weight."

Florence folded her arms across her chest. "What do you weigh then?"

"I don't weigh myself. I don't know. I'm not that thin, though. I don't know why you keep thinking I'm so thin. It's just, I'm very tense. The bike helps me with the stress."

Florence laughed, an ugly, barking sound. "What do you have to be stressed out about? You're the kid. I'm the one with stress."

Emily started to cry. She stood there with her arms around herself, staring at Florence and crying. It was so awful seeing her like that—her face so angry, hopeless and contorted—I didn't know whether to leave the room or go over and say something. But then Florence went and put her arms around Emily. It was like she was hugging a stick; that's how stiff Emily was. "I didn't want to do it, sweetheart," Florence kept saying. "I wish I didn't have to do it."

When Florence left, I followed Emily to her room.

"Stay out," she said when I knocked. I opened the door anyway. I'd thought she'd be facedown on the bed, crying, but she was in the middle of the room, her eyes absolutely dry, doing jumping jacks.

I sat down on the bed. She kept on jumping. "I thought we should get the hell out of here, take a walk or something. . . ."

"How could you let her do it?" She was clapping her hands together so hard it had to hurt. "How could you let her just take it away like that?"

"Me?" I said. "What was I supposed to do?"

"I don't know. Stop her." Her face was very red. "You must have known. You're her big advisor. She tells you everything." She stopped jumping and went over to her bookshelf and started correcting her dolls' posture. "What good are you? You're no help at all."

"That's not fair!" I said, even as I thought: Oh, God, what if I started all this? If I'd let things be, maybe none of this would have happened.

But before I could say anything, Florence barreled in. "You have ten minutes to wash up," she said. "We're going downtown. I made an appointment for you with Dr. Bowman." She'd changed into this serious blue print dress and navy blue pumps with little bows on them. She looked like she'd decided to dress up as Somebody's Mother. Which made me really nervous.

"Who is he?" Emily said. Since the dolls refused to stand up properly, she'd begun rearranging them in order by descending size.

"Your father's doctor. I just called. He's kindly agreed to squeeze us in." She was even talking like Somebody's Mother. She sat down on the end of the bed and smoothed her skirt. "Your father and I had a long chat last night," she said. "I told him you're doing really well. I told him you've been eating nicely."

"So then why are you doing this?" Emily said. She still wasn't looking at us. "You want me to eat more? Give me back my exercise bike and I'll eat more. I promise. I'll eat anything you say. I'll eat right now."

"He wants to come over here."

"He does?" Emily turned around. "When?" she said. I could have sworn I heard excitement in her voice.

"Don't worry," Florence said. "He's not coming. I made it very clear that we can handle this ourselves."

"What'd he say?"

"That's one reason I promised him we'd try his doctor. He thinks this doctor will be tougher. He thinks he'll be able to tell us what to do." She checked her watch. "Come on. Change your clothes. I want you to put on something nice."

"When you leave," Emily said.

"For God's sake, Emily," Florence said, not budging. "We're in a hurry. Take off your goddamn clothes."

"Not with you here."

I got up, but Florence stayed. "You're being ridiculous. I've seen your body a million times. I've changed your diapers. It's like my own body."

"No!" Emily yelled.

This was too much for me. I left the room.

By the time Florence finally got Emily out of the apartment, my head was spinning. I wished I was religious so I'd have someone to pray to who could straighten all this out. Instead, I went to the kitchen and ate some soggy cream puffs, some gluey sesame noodles, and a cold goat cheese and sun-dried tomato minipizza, which was a big mistake. I looked briefly at Emily's Party Possibles chart, said screw it, grabbed my wallet and keys and took a walk.

It started as a walk but as soon as I cut into Central Park, I saw all these people running in the road—no cars, just joggers and bicyclers and roller bladers—and I got this overwhelming urge to run. In gym, I'm one of the kids the gym teacher is always screaming hustle! at, but today I was, like, jet-propelled.

Aside from grocery shopping, my only exercise all week had been cleaning. I thought about how as soon as I got one thing cleaned up, Florence would mess up something else. Before I knew it, my feet began beating out a rhythm: Not-Me-Not-Sarah. Not-Me-Not-Sarah. I remembered my mother warning me—it seemed like months ago—not to let Florence turn me into a maid. Get-A-Maid. Get-A-Maid, my feet told Florence. There were a ton of better things they could have picked to say to Florence, but I guess we all start somewhere. I had a huge stitch in my side but I raised my arms and ran through it. I'd tell her when I got back. I didn't have to clean her apartment.

I untucked my shirt and wiped my face. I wondered if Emily's dad was as bad as Florence. It sounded to me as if Emily wanted to see him.

I ran till my eyes began to blur. Then I limped out of the park and went and got my ears pierced. That implies more of a plan than I had. What I actually did was wander around, drinking a soda I'd bought on the street, looking in store windows and thinking about what I was going to say to Florence. And when I came to this jewelry store with great earrings and a sign that said Yes, We Do Ear Piercing, I walked in.

You might wonder how I'd managed to get to the age of fifteen without getting my ears pierced. The answer is that in the fourth grade, when everyone I knew was getting her ears pierced, my mother and my sister got it done. They got matching little diamond studs. The last thing I wanted, even then, was to be like them. But now, suddenly, I felt like I needed some decoration.

"How many holes are we making today?" the lady in the store asked. She was small and round and had false eyelashes.

"I don't know," I said, examining the earrings in the glass display case. "Two, I guess." A minute ago I hadn't known I was getting any. "To start, anyway." I picked out my studs. I held my hair back and the lady leaned over the counter and marked little *X*'s on my ears in pen. Then she took out this sort of staple gun and held it to my ear. I felt a flash of fear. "Is it going to hurt?"

She shook her head. "We do it to little babies." I felt a quick zap, and an instant later, they were in.

"Let me see." I practically grabbed the hand mirror from her. "Oh, they're nice," I said. "I do look a little different. I look nice." You look great, I heard Angel saying. "How long before I can wear ones like that?" I asked, pointing to a rack filled with beautiful, long earrings with glass beads that glowed like jewels.

"A month, at least," the lady said. She handed me this little ear care booklet and started her speech about cleaning with alcohol and bacitracin. I wasn't listening because I was thinking about all the earrings I was going to buy. I had two whole weeks' pay right in my wallet. I bought a deep blue pair and another with clusters of red and purple beads like tiny grapes. I could hardly wait to get back to the apartment and put my hair up and hold them up against my ears.

I'd already paid for them when I spotted a pair of silver wires with tiny dangling bicycles. "How much?" I asked.

"Eighteen," the lady said.

"I'll take those, too," I said, and bought them for Emily.

CHAPTER 11

I didn't give Emily the earrings that afternoon. When she and Florence got back from the doctor, she went straight to her room and closed the door. I followed Florence to the living room. "How is she?" I asked.

Florence flopped into a chair and kicked her shoes off, groaning. "Never wear high heels," she said. "I don't care how great they make your legs look. They're death." She massaged her foot, then pinched the crease between her eyebrows. "First of all, he kept us waiting for an hour and a half. By which time, needless to say, we were a wreck. Then, he spends all of five minutes with her and presumes to tell me. . . ."

"Is she okay?" I hovered over her. "Florence, does he think she's really—"

"Don't say it!" Florence's eyes flared up behind her glasses. "I hate that word! I am so sick of it. She is not an an-o-rex-ic, or an an-o-rec-tic, or any other category. She's my daughter, who happens to be having a bad time. She's not crazy. It's always the mother's fault. The mother's the sick one, the one killing her child. And of course, I get no credit whatsoever for getting her to eat, which I have. With your help." She tried to smile, but I could see she was fighting to hold herself together.

I sat down across from her. "What did he say?"

Her laugh came out a half snort. "Big surprise. He told her she'd better start eating right away. And he told me to make sure she does."

"But how?"

"You think I know?" Florence said. "The man was an idiot. A complete and utter nincompoop. Which is exactly what I could have expected from Elliott. He even looked like Elliott, the way he glues his hair across his bald spot, as if that fools anybody. And now we've wasted an entire day and she's mad and you think I'm crazy and a rotten mother."

"No," I said, fiddling with my earring. "But you shouldn't have taken away the bike."

"What was I supposed to do?" Florence said. "She's on the damn thing all day long, and Elliott's putting a lot of pressure on me. . . ."

I had the horrible feeling she was going to cry. "But don't you see?" I said. "If you take the bike, she'll just do thousands of jumping jacks, or push-ups. It's part of the whole thing. You must have read about that."

"I've got to get out of these clothes," she said, suddenly standing up. "Do me a huge favor, sweetheart, and unzip me." I helped her with the zipper, but it made me really uncomfortable, being that close to her. "He also said she needs a shrink," she said, her back still to me. "He called up and made an appointment for us. For Thursday."

"Oh, yeah?" I said.

"Nine A.M." She said it like it was a date with the executioner. "It's someone who specializes in girls like Emily."

"And you're going?" I was afraid to hope.

"Do we have a choice?"

This huge relief washed over me. "So then maybe it doesn't matter that he was a nincompoop."

"Tell Emily that," Florence said, as she started toward her room. "She's not speaking to me."

Emily didn't come out for dinner, even though Florence begged her and begged me to beg her, which I wouldn't do. Right after dinner, Florence disappeared into her own room, too. I spent some time messing with my hair, but I'd already tried out every hairstyle that showed my ears, while I waited for them to get home. Pierced ears are great, but if you can't change your earrings, and you've got no one to show them to, they don't do that much to change your life. I watched out the window as two guys got into a big fight over a parking space. I listened to the rooster man's nightly serenade. I thought about things I could say to Emily.

It was pretty late when I opened her door. Her room was empty, so I tried the kitchen. I found her sitting at the table with a glass of diet Sprite and a pile of pink, green, orange, and yellow tablets. "God, Emily, what are you doing?" I said.

"Eating," she said, giving me a look like, how dumb can you get? "That's what I'm supposed to be doing, right?"

"Eating what?" I said.

"Tums," she said.

"You must have major acid indigestion."

"The doctor told me I need calcium," she said. "So these are calcium."

I got a glass and poured myself some soda. "You didn't miss much of a dinner. We just nuked Party Possibles. The egg rolls got about a four but the stuffed mushrooms were a gross minus."

She glanced over at the fridge. "You forgot to put them on the chart." She ate another Tum.

"We were upset," I said. She wet her finger in her soda and ran it round and round her glass till it gave off a high squeal. "I heard you guys really hated that doctor." She rubbed faster and the sound got even louder. "I went for a run," I said. "While you guys were gone. In Central Park." Emily stopped rubbing the glass and stacked the Tums into a little pile. "It was great. I ran at least a mile. I loved it." I thought about mentioning the earrings, but it didn't seem like the right time. I took the top Tum and chewed it up. "Oh, gross! I thought green was mint!"

"They're tutti-frutti," Emily said. "I like them."

"So what I was thinking was, maybe you'd want to go for a run with me tomorrow."

"I'm not allowed. She took away the bike, remember?"

"Right, and in case you don't know it, I told her what I thought of that. But going for a jog with me is not the same as pedaling your brains out in your room." I hoped that was true.

She ate another Tum and made a face. "You're right about these Tums. They're not that great. Do you think she'll let me?"

"Do we care?" I said. "We can just tell her we're going to the park. She's not going to say no to that."

That's how it got left. The next morning, we were all sitting at breakfast, Florence acting nicey-cheerful, Emily fiddling with her toast, when the phone rang. Florence brought it over to the table. She listened for a minute. "That's terrific," she said, smiling. "That's wonderful. Emily'll be absolutely delighted."

"Who was that?" Emily said.

"Mindy Kirlin." Florence was still smiling. "Amanda's coming to the party." Emily's face went totally red. "And the Zimmers aren't going to Long Island until August, so she thinks Alexandra will come, too."

Emily stood up so fast her chair fell over. "You said you wouldn't do that! I hate Amanda and Alexandra. You know they hate me. How could you? You promised me." She ran out of the room. An instant later, her door slammed.

Florence looked at me with glittering eyes. She sighed and blew her breath out. "I thought she'd have a better time if there were kids her age," she said. I kept my mouth shut. I thought about how no matter what she tried, she always got it wrong.

But then Emily was back. "If you still want to do what you said. . . ." She was looking at the ground.

"What's that?" Florence said, eagerly.

"I wasn't talking to you," Emily said. "Sarah, you said if I wanted to go out to the park. . . ."

Florence put her hand on Emily's shoulder. "Sweetheart, everything I do, I'm just trying to make you happy." She looked at me. "You think you girls would like to take a snack?"

Emily said nothing to me in the elevator. I was go-

ing to ask how come she always had to fight with
Florence before she'd go anywhere with me, but she
started running as soon as we hit the street. "Hey, will
you wait up?" I called, as she ran to the corner and
crossed over to the park. After yesterday, my legs did
not want to move. I followed her to this enormous,
fenced-in lake with a running track around it. "Hey
Emily, slow down," I begged. My muscles were so
sore. Plus, it was one of those days when you have to
plow through the air. Even the sea gulls were floating
around as if they were too pooped to fly.

Emily ran me around the entire lake. I walked a
hunk of it, but she kept going, passing people. It's not
surprising, considering she practically lived on the
exercycle. But what surprised me was how pretty she
looked running, like a dancer, or an antelope, small
and delicate and elegant. I'd gotten so used to seeing
her drooping around the house, or fidgeting and edgy,
I'd forgotten how beautiful she seemed when I first
met her. Her legs and arms, which usually seemed so
spindly, moved gracefully, and her face, the few times
I caught up with her, seemed relaxed. I could see why
she wouldn't want to stop. I, on the other hand, was
one big lump of aches and cramps. I did my best to
keep up, but when we passed the water fountain for
the second time, I stopped and stuck my whole head
under the tap.

"*Whew!*" Water streamed off my face. I wiped it on my shirt and flopped down on a bench.

"You're stopping," Emily said, jogging in place. Her face was red but she wasn't winded.

"It's that or die," I said. "I'm sopping." After a while, I hauled myself to my feet and we started home. Now I was feeling pretty good. "You know, if I did this all the time, I'd really get in shape," I said.

"I'll do it," Emily said. "I'll go tomorrow."

"Forget it!" I said. She looked upset. "Come on. (a) My legs can't take it, and (b) it's not good for you to do it every day. But we can go the day after, when you come back from the shrink."

"I don't need a shrink," she said. "I just need to run. That's what makes me feel better, not talking to some stupid doctor."

"Maybe he won't be stupid," I said. "Or maybe it's a woman."

"Hey, baby!" Two guys on bikes made a big circle around us, making kissing noises.

Emily moved closer to me. "It's okay," I said, loudly. "They're just jerks." They rode off, laughing. I rummaged in my pocket for a rubber band and pulled my wet hair into a ponytail. Then I remembered. "Notice anything new and different about me?" I said.

"Your face is purple," Emily said.

"Aside from that. Look hard. I got my ears pierced

yesterday. While you were at the doctor. I meant to show you." I felt a little embarrassed then, so I said, "Big deal, right? Everyone over the age of six months has got pierced ears."

"Except me," Emily said. "Florence won't let me. I wanted to do it last year, but she said not till I'm thirteen."

"What?" I pushed her hair back. She was right. No holes. "You're not going to believe what an idiotic thing I did. I shouldn't even tell you."

"Tell me."

"While I was in the earring place, yesterday, I saw these earrings, and I just felt like getting them for you. They're bicycles."

"You bought them for me?" Emily said. I nodded. Then neither one of us knew what to say so we didn't say anything.

"There's no point even asking her again about piercing my ears," Emily said, when we were almost home.

"I'll take them back," I said. "Or we'll go after the therapist and get you something else."

"No," Emily said. "You got them for me. I'm keeping them."

CHAPTER 12

So we didn't return the earrings. Emily and I spent most of Thursday in a tree. That's an exaggeration. What it was, actually, was this climbing structure built around a huge old oak, with platforms and firemen's poles and slides, and this tree house-like enclosure at the top. She took me there after we ran, after her first therapy appointment, and again Friday, after the second.

I would have loved it up there, ordinarily—high up, leafy, quiet, away from everything. Every now and then, some little kid would step over us to reach the slide, or a squirrel would leap onto the rail and tilt his head at us, but basically, it was our own private little hideaway. Friday, though, was one of those gray, airless days when you just wait for it to rain. And these therapy appointments had loomed over the entire week. Florence had gotten more and more uptight and Emily had gotten more and more quiet. She'd been there twice, now, and still hadn't said a word about it.

"What are you thinking about?" I asked after we'd been sitting there an hour. Which tells you how uptight I was myself. I can't stand people who ask that. Like my father, who actually says, "a penny for your thoughts," which is almost as obnoxious as people telling you to "smile!"

"Napoleon," she said, tearing a leaf into tiny shreds.

"What exactly about him?"

She shrugged. "I don't know. I was just thinking how his doctor poisoned him with antimony." I don't know what I said to that. Nothing too bright, because she looked at me as if I were the peculiar one. "It's in my book. They weren't trying to poison him. They were trying to cure these excruciating stomach pains. He had cancer or something. So they kept giving him these poison laxatives, which they hid in lemonade."

"That's disgusting," I said. "But what does it have to do with anything?"

"You're the one who wants to know what I was thinking."

Two grubby little boys climbed onto our platform with a bucket full of trucks and pushed past us to the slide. "Excuse you!" Emily said. They sat down, one behind the other, but they didn't slide. "Are you going down or not?" she demanded. One of them lay down so his feet were practically in my lap, and one by one, began to roll trucks down the slide, making loud *vrooming* noises. Emily groaned.

"Ignore them," I said. I heard a distant rumble. "Unless you want to leave. It's going to rain."

"I don't want to leave."

"Then tell me about the shrink. You've been there twice, already. I've been dying to hear."

"What do you want to know?" She looked at me warily.

"I don't know. How is it?"

She waited till the boys had sent the last truck down the slide and had slid down after it. "All right."

"That's a start. Is the person nice?"

"I guess." She pulled off another leaf and began shredding it. "I don't know."

"What kind of person is it?"

She shrugged. "A doctor. I guess he's a psychiatrist."

"Do you have to lie down on a couch, like in cartoons?"

"No."

"So when are you going back?" I tried to sound casual.

"I don't know. He said Monday."

I stood up and leaned out over the wall. "Oh, this is great. This is really fun for me. I feel like I'm my mother, trying to pry information out of me."

The playground was one gigantic sandbox, criss-crossed with ramps and bridges and swarming with little kids. Around the outside, moms and baby-sitters sat on benches crowded with strollers and pails and toys. There were some girls my age—mothers' help-ers—digging in the sand with little kids. It pissed me off, suddenly, that all their kids were plump and happy and normal-looking. I'd seen a few of them eyeing me and Emily when we came in. I knew how they must see her—white, stick-like arms and bony legs, stub-born, unhappy mouth, too-big eyes. I had the sudden urge to buy six hot dogs and stuff them down her throat.

"He said I don't have to tell anyone anything," she said.

"Fine," I said.

"He said it's private, between him and me."

"I get the point." I heard another crack of thunder, closer this time. The leaves began to rustle. "It's about to rain," I said. I slid down the slide. My sweaty legs stuck to the hot metal.

Emily slid down after me. "You're mad at me," she said.

"I'm not mad at you." More thunder, then a giant flash of lightning, then another. Gusts of wind blew sand around our legs. Moms threw sand toys into strollers and dragged kids toward the gate. "Let's get out of here," I said.

A minute later, it was total downpour. I grabbed Emily's hand and we began to run. The park was full of people, running, skating, biking toward the exit. Emily broke away and ran ahead. Water streamed down my neck. It squished inside my shoes. "Wait up, will you!" I yelled to Emily. We ran down Central Park West. A man ran past me carrying his dog. At last I saw our building.

"Yo, *Flaca!* Over here!" It was Angel, running toward us with the doorman's huge umbrella. "Come under here!" he called. We crowded under so I was pressed up right against him. "I saw you two running and I said, 'Let me see if I can give them a little shelter from the storm.'"

"Thanks," I said, looking up into his eyes. Which made my face instantly go out of control, so I looked away.

"Let's go in this way." He hurried us down a ramp and through a metal door into the basement. "Come in here. I'll give you a towel." We went around a corner, then up two steps into this little room with a scratched-up desk littered with papers and old coffee cups, and some chairs that looked like stuff people had thrown away. Over the desk was a hardware store calendar with a picture of two ladies in red-and-black tasseled underwear.

"That's a little gross," I said.

"Sorry about that," Angel said. "My father's taste. This is his office. Have a seat." I sat. He reached in a cabinet and gave us each a towel. Then he sat down, leaned his chair back on two legs and smiled at me. "I was just thinking about you," he said. "I'm like, when am I going to see Sarah, and here you are. It must be fate."

I had to bury my face in the towel so he wouldn't see me blush.

Emily was still standing by the door, water dripping from her hair. "Man, you look terrible," Angel said to her. She put a hand up to her hair. "You should see yourself. The original drowned rat."

"I can leave," she said. "I'm sure there are enough rats in the basement without me around."

"Whoa." Angel shook his finger at her. "Better not let my dad hear you."

"Emily, don't be ridiculous," I said.

"I have things to do anyway," she said.

"What things?" I said.

But Angel just said, "Okay, *Flaca*, see you around."

"I guess I should go then, too," I said, standing.

"What for?" Angel said. "Sit here and dry off. I'm not doing anything. You want some coffee or something?"

I felt my blood buzzing through my veins. "I'll be up in a minute," I said to Emily.

"What's that name you keep calling her?" I said after she'd left.

"*Flaca*. Means skinny. Don't stand there. Sit."

"I don't think you should say that to her," I said, sitting down again. "That's probably why she was so touchy. She has a real problem, you know?"

"Nah. Emily and I go way back. She knows I'm joking with her. I always tease her. It's good for her." He got up and went over to the window ledge, setting up the coffee maker. "It's not good to take yourself so seriously. Makes you old before your time." He got some water from the cooler, then measured coffee from a yellow bag. "I'm just making a small pot. It'll take a minute. Spanish coffee. Ever had it?" I shook my head. "Strong and sweet. Like me." He made a silly face, which made me like him even more. "Did Ms. Friedman tell you she wants me to help out at some party next week?"

"Are you going to do it?" I said. He nodded. Then, trying even harder to sound normal, I asked, "What does she want you to do?"

"Sing, dance, juggle."

I giggled. "No, seriously."

"Everyone's so serious. Hang out witchoo. What-ever."

I giggled again.

"What's funny?"

"The way you say 'witchoo.' Like you're sneezing or something."

"Hey, I'm from the Bronx." He poured two mugs of coffee, spooned in some sugar and handed one to me. I took a tiny sip. It was so strong I thought it would melt the enamel off my teeth, but it was really good—sweet and rich and bitter all at once. The total opposite of the decaf pond water my parents drink.

"How is it?" He leaned toward me.

"It's great. I love it," I said, then felt my face go red again because that sounded so personal.

We sat there without saying anything, just drinking. Then Angel tipped his chair back again, looking right into my eyes. "I watch people, you know. It's one of my things, watching people."

"Me, too," I said. "I study everyone."

"I studied you."

"You've hardly even seen me."

"I've seen you enough."

What I wanted to say was: What do you see? But instead I looked into my cup to check if I had any coffee left.

He got the pot and poured us both some more. I was hoping he'd keep talking about me, even though it made me nervous, but instead he said, after he sat down, "You take people up and down in the elevator a few times, you find out stuff. Some people, it's like you're part of the machinery, they don't see you, even. They'll like, pick their nose or something, like they're by themself. Other people, forget it. They'll tell you anything."

"Like what?"

"Personal stuff. You name it. Troubles with their husbands, with the job, the maid, the kids. Stuff you don't want to know. Specially when I'm working nights, which I am now. They'll keep you standing there telling you their life story while tenants on the other floors are leaning on the buzzer."

"Does Florence tell you stuff?"

"Sure, all the time."

"About Emily or about Elliott?"

"Both. Him mostly, before he left. He looked like an okay guy, compared to some, but you should have heard her."

"What'd she say?" I was dying to know more about Elliott.

"Oh, the usual complaints. Now it's mostly about Emily. So I know she's got problems. I mean, you just have to look at her. I feel kinda bad for her. She was always a quiet kid, but she'd like, joke around with me. Plus, even last summer, when I worked days, I'd see her girlfriends come over. She was more like a kid. What is she now, eleven?"

"Twelve."

"And you?"

"Fifteen." It came out before I thought. I could have shot myself. Fifteen was so humiliating. There was no way you could not notice I was closer to Emily's age than to his. I took a big gulp of my coffee. It burned the whole way down. I stood up. "I've got to get going," I said.

"You're not going to keep me company?"

"I really have to go," I said, feeling this gray gloom close over me.

"Okay then. See you next Friday night, or hopefully, before. You'll be there for the party, right?"

"I'll be there." I just wanted to get away.

But then, as I rode up in the elevator, I started thinking about the way he looked at me, and I said, wait a minute. I'm no dummy. I may be fifteen, and I may not be a People Person, but I can tell when someone likes me.

CHAPTER 13

By the time I got to the apartment, I'd cheered up. Partly, it was imagining calling my grandmother, who is an even bigger snob than my parents, and telling her, "I'm in love with an elevator man named Angel," and her saying, "Angel? What kind of name is Angel? He's not Puerto Rican, is he?" It was a great thought, but that wasn't really what I wanted. What I wanted was someone nice to say his name out loud to, someone to discuss him with. Someone who'd be happy for me.

That sure wasn't Florence. The minute I came in, she started ranting about how her birthday party was in one week and no one had anything to wear, and how we'd cleaned but now everything was totally messed up again, and how her life was out of control and nobody was helping. So I finally said it. "Get a maid," I said. "Call up a cleaning service. It will make us all much happier."

"I don't know any maids," she said, looking pissed and interested at the same time, as if she didn't like being told how to run her life but knew I had a good idea.

"Ask people you know, then," I said. "Or look in the yellow pages. Here." I pulled the phone book from the shelf and paged through till I found the listing. "Listen to this. 'House a Mess? Call us. We're Maid to Clean.' " I read her the number.

A half hour later, she knocked on my door and reported that Maid to Clean was sending a whole team the day before the party. And now I was her dearest friend. I was so terrific. She didn't know what she'd do without me. Which gave me the urge to go in and see if Emily had cheered up any.

I got a drink and nuked myself an egg roll and brought it to her room. "Angel likes you a lot," I said. "He says you're very nice."

She was lying on the floor with her feet up on the wall, not reading or anything, just lying there. "He's saying that because he likes you. You're the one he likes," she said.

My heart *boinged*. "You think so?" I was trying to sound like it was purely intellectual curiosity.

"*Duh*."

I sat down next to her. "No, seriously. Do you really think he likes me?" She pushed away from the wall, propped her hands on her waist, raised her hips up off the floor, and started doing pedaling exercises.

"You look so weird that way, with your chin squashed up against your neck. How old do you think he is?"

"Who?" she said.

"Angel, you dummy!"

"Twenty-five."

"C'mon Emily. He is not twenty-five." Praying she was just giving me a hard time. "Guess what. Our cleaning days are over." I told her about Maid to Clean. "A stroke of genius, right? You have to admit, your friend here is pretty smart."

"Would you mind taking that greasy egg roll out of here," she said. "It's starting to make me sick."

"Well, pardon me for living," I said. I got up and headed for the door. "Why I even wanted to come in here is beyond me."

She didn't come to dinner. She'd told Florence that the therapist—whose name, I finally found out, was Dr. Kahn—said it was fine if she wanted to eat alone, so she brought her turkey cutlet and baked potato and carrots to her room. It didn't bother me one bit.

She did show up at breakfast the next morning, though, as Florence and I were finishing our coffee. I'd decided I now drank coffee. Hers wasn't as good as Angel's, but I liked having a mug to hold and it helped give me back that cool, grown-up feeling. Or maybe that was the caffeine.

"So." Florence was carefully cheerful. She swallowed her last bite of toast and wiped her mouth. "We solved the cleaning. Now we just have to find Emily a dress."

"Why do I need a dress?" Emily said. She seemed to have developed a new eating method: fishing her Cheerios out one by one so no milk came along with them, then nibbling them up without her lips touching the spoon. It was extremely irritating.

"So you'll look festive," Florence said. "Like a normal kid, at a normal party."

"Instead of what?" Emily said.

"Oh Emily," Florence sighed, "can't you indulge me, just this once? I really want you to have a dress. It'll be my birthday present."

"I already got you a present," Emily said. "I got you a good present." I remembered the fancy soaps.

"This is the only present I want. To see you in a

lovely dress." Florence suddenly stood up and clapped her hands. "I have the best idea! We'll get Sarah a dress, too. I know exactly where we'll go. Right down here on Columbus, what's-its-name, you know, that one that always has those darling dresses in the window."

"I'm not really the darling dress type," I said. "I don't even wear dresses. Last time I wore a dress was at eighth grade graduation."

"Then it's about time you had one." She brought her place mat over to the sink, in the process knocking all the crumbs off onto the floor. "Not to worry." She spread her arms expansively. "Maid to Clean will clean it up." She turned to me. "We'll get you both new dresses. My treat. You'll be gorgeous."

Dubious, I thought. But as we were walking down Columbus Avenue, past all the store windows, I found myself getting all excited. I wanted everything I saw: the crazy jumpsuits, leopard sandals, alligator cowboy boots, lacy underwear—things I'd never seen before and never in a million years would wear. Looking at things and thinking: that's something I bet Angel would like.

You have to understand, I'm generally not into acquisitions. I avoid the mall. I'll buy something if I need it, like new jeans or a new jacket, but don't ask me to, like, shop for entertainment. And ordinarily I'd have found the store Florence took us into totally intimidating. It was one of those places with the really high ceilings and wall-to-wall carpets, where the salesladies introduce themselves when you come in and follow you around asking, May I help you?

I immediately spotted these incredible flowered dresses—not little, dippy flowers, like the graduation dress my mother made me buy, but wild, funky, outrageous flowers. Outrageous and expensive. I could hardly believe Florence would buy me something here. But while Emily squatted against the wall and closed her eyes as if she might fall asleep at any moment, Florence and I began flipping through the racks. The saleswoman, Yvonne, helped me find my size and carried the dresses to the dressing room. I threw off my old stretched-out shirt and khaki shorts and pulled the first dress over my head. It was made of this thin, silky material in purplish, dusky colors that made my eyes look very bright. It fit perfectly. And it had total class, but it wasn't just that. Something about this dress, it made me look slim and curvy at the same time. This is it, I thought as I turned in front of the mirror. This is what I was meant to look like.

"*Ta-da!*" I said, as I stepped out of the dressing room. I pushed my hair back, glad again I'd had my ears pierced. I couldn't get over how good I looked. I absolutely did not look fifteen.

"Look at you!" Florence declared. "What a transformation! You're a knockout." I heard Angel saying it: "You're a knockout!"

The saleswoman nodded. "It's perfect."

Emily opened her eyes and looked at me for a long time, but I couldn't tell what she was thinking.

I went back in and tried on the others, but the green made me look slightly embalmed and the white seemed too much like a nightgown. It was definitely the purple, but I came back out to check what else they had.

Florence, looking totally exasperated, was holding a red dress in front of Emily. "Well, what about this one, then?" she was saying. There was a huge pile of dresses on the bench beside her.

Emily, standing up now, shook her head. "I don't wear colors like that."

"That's the whole point. Try it." Florence gave the saleswoman a toothy, phony smile.

"I don't like it," Emily said.

"Then find one you do like. You haven't even looked."

"I can see from here."

"Well, we're not leaving without a dress," Florence said.

By now, I'd found even more possibilities, so I went back to try them on. This time, when I came out, Emily was slouched in front of the three-way mirror in

the red dress, making throw-up faces at herself. The
bright red actually looked nice with her dark eyes, but
the dress drooped down to her ankles and the puffy
sleeves and low neckline made her collarbone look
really sharp. "Why can't I just wear my white one?"
she was saying. "That one with the little dots."

"Oh, for God's sake," Florence snapped. "You wore
that dress when you were eight. It'll come up to your
bellybutton."

"I think this four might be a bit too big." The saleswoman stepped over to Emily and adjusted the shoulder pads. "I'll see if we have a two."

"Size two!" Florence exclaimed. "I've never even
made it to the single digits." I couldn't tell if she was
upset that Emily needed so small a size, or proud, or
jealous.

In any case, I was having a great time, so I went
back to the dressing room and tried on another dress.
I would never have picked this one, but the saleswoman insisted it looked really great on. "Oh, that's so
cute!" she said, when I came out. "I think I like this
one the best."

"It's too pink," I said. "And fluffy. I can't handle
pink and fluffy."

Now Emily emerged from the dressing room in a
stretchy orange and yellow minidress. "See, I look
grotesque," she said, tugging at the hem.

"You don't," Florence said. "Anyway, what do you expect? You're skin and bone."

"How can you say that?" Emily pinched her thigh. "Look at this pudge. Look at this fat above my knees."

"Emily," Florence said. "That's what legs look like. You're a woman. Women's legs are supposed to have flesh on them."

"*Icch!*" Emily shuddered.

"Emily," Florence was yelling now. "I'm getting cranky. We're getting a dress and that's that. Yvonne has shown you dozens. Now pick."

"But I don't like any of them."

This scene was feeling even worse than mealtime. Plus, I felt like an idiot in the pink tutu, so I went back to try the purple dress one more time. There was no question. It was definitely my new dress.

When I came out, still wearing it, Emily had changed again and was standing with her arms folded and her chin out, staring sullenly at Florence, who looked about to scream.

"May I make a suggestion?" the saleswoman said. "I think Emily would look very cute in this little dress her sister's wearing. And I think I have it in a two. Shall I go check?"

I am not related to this person. This little creep is *not* my sister. I almost said it. But Emily was looking at me and she seemed so pathetic and expectant, suddenly, that I couldn't.

"I'll be happy to check," the saleswoman said again.

What was it with these Friedmans that everyone wanted so badly to solve their problems?

"What an absolutely great idea!" Florence said. "I don't suppose you have one in my size, too, so we could all be sisters. Just joking! But I do love the idea of the two of you in matching dresses. What do you think Emily?" She was smiling now. "Isn't it a good idea?"

I thought that would be the kiss of death. But the saleswoman brought the dress, and Emily held it up against herself, and then, for an instant, our eyes met in the mirror. "It looks okay," she said.

"I thought you wouldn't wear colors," Florence said. "I thought you were the girl who wanted to wear her baby dress."

"No," Emily said. "I'll get one like Sarah's."

CHAPTER 14

"So are you going to put it on?" I said, when we got home. She'd refused to try the dress on in the store. I'd put mine on again to check out how it looked with my new shoes, which we'd gotten in another fancy store on the way home. I'd turned Emily's radio on and was dancing around her room. Lest you were wondering, I'm not someone who can dance. I'm someone who avoids school dances, who lurks in corners at weddings and bar mitzvahs, who heads for the hills whenever her sister starts to dance around the living room. Something about dancing, it just feels too Out There. This dress, though, was definitely a dancer's dress. Plus, I absolutely loved my shoes, suede ballet slippers in almost the exact same shade of purple. They'd cost me an entire week's pay, but they made me feel long-legged and delicate and elegant. Like Emily, in fact.

I boogied past her to the mirror. She was straightening her animals, acting like she didn't know me. "I think Angel is really going to like this outfit," I said, studying my legs. When she didn't say anything, I added, "He'll love that we're both wearing it." I should have given it up right there. Instead, I kept bugging her to put the dress on and dance with me. "C'mon," I kept saying. "If I can handle a new image, you can. Put it on. We'll be the Fabulous Schmidlap Sisters." Don't ask why I said that, except there's a man named Mr. Schmidlap down the road from us. I struck a pose. "And now, ladies and gentlemen, direct from Las Vegas, or perhaps, the moon, I bring you . . ."

Emily clicked off the radio and stood there, staring at me. I felt, all of a sudden, like in this dream I have sometimes, where I'm at school, up on the stage in front of everybody, and I look down and realize I forgot to put on any clothes.

Then Florence came in, all eager and smiley, saying, "Is this a private party?" and the cold, hollow feeling in my stomach got even worse. I was being just like Florence. Trying too hard. Deluding myself I was just this carefree kid with a possible boyfriend, and a sexy new dress, and a friend who was just giving me a hard time.

Emily took her food to her room again that night. She brought her plate back herself, so I couldn't tell how much she ate. I had an impulse to call my sister and tell her about my new things, but I was afraid if I did, my mother would get on the phone and I'd either have to lie or admit that things were bad.

Monday morning, while they went to Dr. Kahn, I took the laundry to the basement. I waited there the whole time, thinking Angel might go by, but the only person I saw was Mr. Farber, in his suit, as usual. "So where's my sweet little Emily today?" he said.

"At the psychiatrist," I said.

He clicked his tongue against his teeth. "Such a nice girl. Such a shame. My wife has mental problems, too. You learn to live with it. What else can you do?"

"We've gotta do something," I said. "I just hope this Dr. Kahn is doing something."

When they got home, Emily went to her room, as usual. I followed Florence to the kitchen. She stood, staring into the open refrigerator, saying nothing. Then she closed the refrigerator, dragged a chair over to the cabinets, climbed up, ripped off the Florence Fortitude sign on the top shelf and took down the box of Mallomars. "Screw the diet," she said. "I need some comfort food. I definitely need some comfort." She had the box open before she'd even climbed off the chair, not noticing, luckily, all the ones I'd eaten. She crammed one in her mouth and held the box out. I took one. She poured us both a glass of milk.

"I hate milk," I said, but she'd decided we both needed comfort.

"He doesn't talk to me, this so-called therapist," she said when we'd sat down. "I don't even go into his office. It's supposed to be her thing, nothing to do with me. I find out nothing except what she deigns to tell me."

"Which is?" I pushed my milk away.

"That he says she doesn't have to talk to me."

By now, she'd eaten almost all the cookies. "It's not working," she said.

"What?" I asked.

"I read in some magazine once, that it's biologically impossible to be anxious while you're chewing, but it's not true. A thousand calories later and I'm just as anxious."

She wasn't the only anxious one. As the week went on, I got terminally grouchy. I couldn't tell how Emily was doing, since she spent most of her time in her room. There was no incentive for her to come out, because each time she did, Florence was bugging her: smiling too hard and starting sentences with "Look how Sarah . . . ," or "Sarah always . . . ," or "Sarah never . . ." or, in her other mode, yelling, "You were a lot easier to get along with before this shrink person got a hold of you!"

One afternoon, Emily did tell me she wanted to go out for a run. I thought it was perverse of her, since it was ninety-five degrees and muggy as a steam bath, but I went. She ran ahead of me the whole way and then was mad because I refused to let her go around the reservoir a second time. Then she was mad because I didn't feel like going to the broiling hot playground and sitting in the tree. So when we got home, she went straight back to her room again.

By the time the cleaners came, Thursday, I thought we all might kill each other.

From the name Maid to Clean, I'd been picturing old ladies in aprons, carrying pails and mops, but at eight A.M., three guys showed up. Young, greatlooking guys.

"Thank God you've come!" Florence said. "Oh, organize me, please! I'm counting on you three to put some order in my life." You'd never have guessed that minutes before, she'd been having a conniption, telling Emily to stop fishing for her Cheerios and finish her damn breakfast, yelling at me to get everything out of sight before the cleaners came, it didn't matter where, just stuff it somewhere, in a closet, anywhere.

I tried not to stare as they unloaded a cart filled with cleaning equipment. They were all tall and handsome, like guys you'd see on TV commercials, super clean-cut in ironed jeans and T-shirts. One of them winked at me and I blushed like a lunatic.

"You gentlemen look like actors," Florence said, when they'd introduced themselves as Darrell, Bruce, and Fitz. Darrell, the black one, nodded. "Have I seen you in anything?"

"Perhaps," he said, in a deep, actory voice.

"We do off-Broadway mostly," Bruce, the one who had winked, said. He had a southern accent that I really liked.

"Did you hear that, Emily, they're actors?" Florence was actually fluttering her eyelashes. "I knew you looked like actors. My daughter, Emily, is very interested in theater. She also dances." Emily, who'd been edging toward her room, gave Florence a murderous look.

"And I'm a writer," Florence said. "A novelist, actually. That's why the place is a tad messy. . . ."

"And what about you?" Bruce said to me.

"Uh, duh," I said. Not really, but it felt like that.

"Come on, girls, we'd better go so they can get to work," Florence said, showing no inclination to leave. "We'll go out somewhere and leave them the apartment." She turned to them. "Now, do a good job. There'll be guests swarming absolutely everywhere tomorrow. You know how friends are, looking in closets, peeping into cupboards. . . ." I thought she was probably joking, but Emily tugged at her arm and whispered something. "Emily's worried you'll mess up her things," Florence said, still smiling. "She's very particular."

"Please! Don't let them in my room," Emily said. "I'll clean it myself, okay?" She looked almost panicky even though her room was the only clean place in the house.

"Fine," Florence said. "You clean your room. Sarah and I'll go out."

Emily went to guard her room. Florence went to get her shoes. So there I was, watching these guys put on aprons and gloves, and next thing I know, I'm saying, "Can I help?"

Bruce said he was the kitchen man and always worked alone, but Darrell handed me a dust mop and a pair of rubber gloves, and when Florence came back, newly lipsticked, with her purse, I told her I was staying.

We did the foyer first. Fitz pushed furniture, Darrell vacuumed, and I did what Florence had said—shoved stuff into drawers and closets: gloves, scarves, tennis balls, old mail, the broken answering machine, umbrellas, worn-out purses. I didn't care where I crammed them, just so they were out of sight.

The guys worked fast and at first, nobody said much. I didn't care. I was elated to be around (a) males, (b) cute males, but mainly regular, cheerful energetic human beings. We went on to the living room, piling up newspapers and magazines, cleaning behind stuff and under stuff, pulling the cushions off the couches, rolling up the rugs. It was truly amazing, the pencils, rubber bands, old bank statements, and general debris lurking beneath those rugs.

"Aha!" Fitz uncovered an ancient Milk-Bone.

"But there's no dog here," I said.

Fitz pointed his finger like a teacher. "Fitz's rule: There's always a dog biscuit. Wherever we go, there is invariably a dog biscuit under the rug."

"God, I wonder if Emily used to have a dog," I said, thinking maybe Elliott took it, wondering if she missed it. There was so much about Emily I didn't know.

"Evidently," Fitz said. He had this funny, drawling way of saying things.

"Is this the messiest apartment you've ever seen?" I asked, looking at the two Lawn and Leaf bags we'd already filled.

"Are you serious?" Darrell set me straight. "You should see some of the places we do. Like this one last week, where the person had just died. . . ."

I realized that wasn't what I'd wanted to ask at all.

What I wanted was an outside opinion. "You see all different apartments, right? Does this place seem, you know, weird in any way?"

"Honey child." This time it was Fitz. "We can tell you weird."

I hesitated. "I don't mean the apartment, I mean, like, the people?"

Fitz snickered. "That lady last week with the cats. . . ."

Darrell chimed in. "She must've had thirty cats."

"And these were weird cats, let me tell you, darling. And that guy who dressed his boa constrictor in a knitted sweater? I mean it was a light blue tube— because his landlord wasn't sending up the heat?"

"I wasn't there," Darrell said. "I left, remember? I draw the line at snakes."

They had me laughing so hard, I forgot about my question. Then, we were in the dining room and Fitz moved this big, ugly blue sort of Chinese urn filled with dried weeds. "Oh, my," he said suddenly, in that same dry, drawling way. "Look in here. Looks like we have a squirrel living here."

My stomach gave a warning lurch.

"Someone's got some bagels and some old rolls stashed in here and, what is this?" He leaned closer. "A petrified potato."

Darrell peered in, then checked the matching urn on

the other side of the chest. "There's food in this one, too," he said, wrinkling his nose. "More bread. Some dead zucchini. And something that looks like it used to be some kind of meat."

This stuff might have been in there a really long time, I told myself. It could be as old as the dog biscuit. It had to have been from before I'd come. I told myself Emily was getting help. She didn't need to do anything like that now. But a sick clammy feeling was rising in my chest.

"I take it back," Fitz said to me. "Someone around here is definitely weird."

Darrell laughed. "Better not look in the umbrella stand. You might find a leg of lamb. . . ."

I didn't laugh. At least I can say that for myself. But I also didn't tell them to shut up. I guess I was still trying to pretend that I was one of them and that this was just another weird story to add to our collection, and that I was what they were: someone Florence had hired for a few hours, someone who could start the job and finish it, and walk away.

CHAPTER 15

After the cleaners left, I went to my room and did not come out. I couldn't face Emily or Florence. At dinnertime, when Florence knocked, I told her through the door that I had cramps. All evening, I stared out my window at the park, praying to the biggest tree that I could see for no more horrible surprises.

I should have picked a different tree.

The day of the party started out okay, considering. The sick feeling came back as I passed the urns on my way to the kitchen for breakfast, but Florence was glad to see me and excited about the party and Emily actually ate half an English muffin and four spoonfuls of cottage cheese, and I started to hope I'd been overreacting. Then they went off to Dr. Kahn and to get Florence's hair done, and I took a long shower and shaved my legs and thought about Angel.

It was after noon when they got back, loaded down with flowers. As usual, Emily went directly to her room. Then the delivery people started coming: first, the grocery guy, then the wine. I was at the kitchen sink, scrubbing flower vases, when the caterer arrived with her helper. Then Angel rang the bell with two big bags of ice.

So there we all were—Florence showing the caterers around, Angel helping unpack the food, me trying to look nonchalant with Angel so close by—when Emily stormed in.

"Who went in my room?" she demanded, her arms folded tight across her chest, her voice trembling with rage. "Who touched something of mine?"

"Not me," I said, immediately feeling guilty without knowing why.

"Hey, I just got here," Angel said, "so it couldn't be me."

"Emily." Florence stopped talking to the caterer. "Emily." She went over and put her hand on Emily's shoulder. "No one's touched your room. No one even wants to."

"I'm not a two year old. Don't talk to me like I'm a two year old who doesn't know anything." She was sputtering. "I know it was you. I hid it and you read it anyway."

"Sweetheart, hid what?" Florence still had on her public smile. "What are you talking about?"

"Stop lying. You know perfectly well. . . . You read my journal. You went into my room and looked through my things and read my private journal."

"I forgot you even had a journal," I said, talking loud to fend off the sick, clammy feeling in my guts.

"Well, my mother didn't forget." She said "my mother" like she meant "my cockroach" or "my leprosy."

Florence looked at me, then at the caterer and blew her breath out. "Would you excuse us, Mary. We're all a bit on edge today."

"No problem." The caterer, who looked like a nice lady, went into the other room. The helper followed. Angel started edging toward the door as well, but the look I gave him must have made him change his mind. I felt a real bad fight brewing and I could not see leaving them alone.

At first, Florence tried denying she'd read the journal. Then she told Emily to calm down, that she wasn't herself today. Then, when she finally admitted that she'd "peeked," she tried to tell Emily she hadn't done anything that bad. "It's not like I even saw anything that personal," she insisted. I had the hideous thought that she might have read my journal too. I left it right there on the desk. And half of what was in it was about her. "All I saw was lists of numbers," she kept saying. "What is it, calorie counts? How secret can that be?"

One minute she was arguing; the next, she was practically pleading. "You don't talk to me. You don't tell me anything anymore. I only did it because I care so much. I only wanted to know what's going on in your mind."

"You're out of control," Emily said. She sounded so supercilious, so sneering and contemptuous, I just knew the words were Elliott's.

And Florence blew. "Who the hell do you think you are?" she screamed. "Do I need a crisis from you just when things are going well?"

Angel looked at my face, then took my arm and steered me toward the kitchen door and led me out to the back hall, with the trash can and the recycling bins. I could still hear every word. "This is supposed to be my night," Florence shrieked. "Don't I deserve a little happiness? I've worked like a dog to make this party happen and you're manufacturing a crisis just to spoil things and I'm not going to let you. You've spoiled enough around here with your craziness. I saw you doing it with Daddy. That's exactly why you stopped eating."

I tried putting my fingers in my ears, but it didn't help.

"You're the one who drove him away," Emily screamed back. "You're the one who turned into a big fat pig."

Angel shook his head and rang for the service elevator. "This is too intense for me," he said. "I'll check back later."

"What'll I do?" I said. "I can't go back in there."

"I wash my hands of you!" Florence hollered. "I'm going to let your father handle this. You can starve yourself to death for all I care."

"Come on with me," Angel said.

I couldn't look at him as we rode down to the basement. I've had plenty of horrendous fights. I've told all of them—my sister and my parents both—I hated them and wanted them to die. But it's different when it's someone else's family, and you have no business hearing it, and no faith that they don't mean the deadly things they say.

We were out on the street before the lump in my throat had dissolved enough for me to talk. "Where are we going?" I said.

"Where do you want to go?"

"Away from here."

So we just started walking. At Seventy-second Street, we turned west and joined the crowds of shoppers and old ladies and mothers pushing strollers. It was another stifling day. The air smelled like fried-chicken grease and old popcorn. "You want a drink or a hot dog or something?" he said, as we reached a crowded hot dog stand. I shook my head, but he pushed his way to the counter and got a hot dog with onions and a large mixed papaya and pina colada. "Sure you don't want something?" He took a huge bite and wiped his mouth. "These hot dogs are good."

I shook my head. I'd had no lunch, but there was still this thick lump filling up my chest.

"I know exactly why she did it," I said as we turned downtown on Broadway, talking to myself as much as to him.

"Did what?" Angel drained his cup, then tossed it into an overflowing trash can.

"Read her journal. Florence, I mean. Not that I'd ever do it." I wasn't sure that was true, but I hoped it was. "I understand it, though. She's just so frustrating, Emily. She makes you want to kill her, sometimes."

"She looks so pathetic," Angel said.

"Exactly! That's the thing. You think, here's this poor pathetic kid. All you want to do is help her get better. And you try and you try and she says, 'Up yours!' "

"I see what you're saying. Like a power thing," Angel said.

"But she's killing herself." I realized I was yelling, but I couldn't stop. "What good is all the power going to do her if she's dead?"

He looked at me. "You're exaggerating, right? I mean, she's not that bad off."

"I don't know," I said. "I thought she was doing better, but now this fight . . . and I thought she was eating more. . . ." I told him about finding the secret stash of food. "I'm scared," I said. "I'm really scared. I'm supposed to be helping her. She has a shrink and everything, but what if it doesn't work?"

When we got to the Fifty-ninth Street subway station, this guy in an orange suit was walking back and forth, handing out cards. He held one out to me, so I took it. It said Mini Storage Can Save Your Life. "Maybe that's what I need," I said, showing it to Angel. "I need something."

He stopped walking. "Listen," he said. "They're the one with the problem. Not you. You can't just let it eat you up."

I made a face. "No pun intended."

"No. Seriously," Angel said. "You gotta ease up. You're as bad as them. You take life too hard."

"What's that, your theme song?" I said. " 'Don't worry, be happy'? Do you sign your name with little smiley faces, too?" As soon as I said it, I was sorry. "Don't mind me," I said. "I'm just totally bummed out. I came here because my life was too boring, nothing happening. Now there's too much happening. And it's all bad."

"Hey. Not all bad," he said. "You met me."

He said it in the usual jokey Angel way, and I responded with my usual sparkling repartee. "What time is it?" I said. "I didn't wear my watch. Hot days like this, I usually don't wear it because it makes my wrist itch." Then, so he would know I knew how dumb I'd sounded, I made a geeky face.

He checked his watch and frowned. "It's late. It's after four. We gotta turn around."

Then an amazing thing happened. Right there on the sidewalk, he put his arms around me and pulled me close. Right there on Broadway, with all these kids and old ladies tromping past, he just stood there, holding me. My heart thumped crazily. First I didn't know what to do with my arms, which were pinned down by my sides, but then I figured out how to get them loose, and I held him tight around his neck. I thought about how as long as I could remember, I'd felt this giant ache whenever I saw couples on the street kissing, or even holding hands. How it felt like it would never happen to me.

"Don't be sad," he said into my neck. "I don't like to

see you sad." I hadn't known I was sad, till he said it. I leaned into him, collapsed against him, let him hold me up. I don't know how long we stood like that. But then he let me go.

I felt like crying.

He cuffed me on the head. "Will you cheer up?" he said.

"I'll try," I said, to please him. We turned around and started walking back uptown. "I don't know why you think things are going to work out," I said.

"Because they do," he said.

"God, you're so nice," I said. "I never met someone so nice." Then I couldn't look at him for about ten blocks.

He didn't seem to notice. He kept asking me questions about the party and what time guests were coming, saying how he needed to go home and shower, saying how Florence was paying him real well and he could use the money, so he couldn't afford to piss her off. As if it was perfectly ordinary to have held me like that in the middle of the street, as if nothing had changed between us. For a minute, I thought I had imagined the whole thing, but I knew I hadn't. Then I started worrying that he didn't think of me that way at all, that it was just some burst of uncle-ish affection. And then we were back outside our building.

He stopped outside the ramp down to the basement, "I'll see you in a bit," he said.

"Oh, God," I said. "You mean I have to face them by myself? You're making me be alone with them?"

He cuffed me on the head again, but this time, kept his hand there. "Stop worrying. You can deal with it. They've probably kissed and made up by now." I rolled my eyes. "Plus, even if they haven't, with all those guests and stuff around, they'll be on good behavior. I promise." He slid his hand down till it rested on my neck. "Plus, in a few minutes, you won't be alone. You'll have me to keep you company."

CHAPTER 16

No sooner was my key in the lock, than Florence flung open the door. But when she saw me, her face darkened. "Oh, it's you," she said. "I thought it might be Emily." She looked up and down the hall. "She's not with you? Have you seen her anywhere?"

I came inside. "What's going on?" I said. Florence's eyes were red and her hair was sticking out like she'd been pulling at it. "Where is Emily?"

"I don't know! She left! I got so mad and now, I've driven her away!" Florence took off her glasses and wiped her eyes, then told me how the fight had made her so upset, she'd had to take two aspirin and lie down. How, when she'd gotten up, she'd had one problem after another with the caterer, and then, when she'd finally knocked on Emily's door, Emily was gone. "You know she never goes anywhere," she said. "And never without telling me or leaving me a note. She was so upset. I'm scared she's run away."

Another crisis was too much for me. I couldn't deal with it.

"Where are you going?" Florence cried as I headed for the door. All I wanted was a break, a quiet time to think about Angel and what had happened and to feel what I was feeling. "You're not going to leave me, too?"

"I'll be right back," I said.

Angel was barefoot, his hair still wet from the shower, when he opened the door of his apartment. "What's up?" he said. He was dressed for working at the party, in black pants and a white shirt. Behind him I could see a short, white-haired lady at the stove.

"Angel, I need you," I said.

"Ooh, baby, I need you, too." Giving me this corny, sexy look. The old lady frowned at him.

"Stop it, Angel, this is serious," I said.

"Oh. That's too bad," he said. But he dropped his joking when I told him what had happened. He said something in Spanish to the old lady, and put on his shoes and we rushed back to the apartment.

I could hear shouts coming from the kitchen as soon as we walked in. "Maybe she's back," I said, but it was only Florence fighting with the caterer.

"Ms. Friedman," Angel said, as if all this were just normal. "What's happ'nin'? Something I can do to help?"

Florence pointed to the counter, which was loaded with bowls and platters of every hors d'oeuvre known to man, as well as this humongous fish paved over with scales made out of sliced radishes and cucumbers. Her face was grim. "Help Mary take the food back out to her car."

"Excuse me?" Angel said.

"The party's off," she said. "I'm canceling the party. So I need this stuff out of here. Mary's upset, which is understandable." She turned to the caterer, who looked about to kill. "It's gorgeous, Mary. That's not the issue. We both know your food is fabulous. I mean, look at it. . . ." Florence pointed to these mounds of miniature vegetables nestled inside ruffly cabbage leaves. "And I'll pay for all of it."

"What's going on?" Angel said.

"My daughter's gone," Florence said. "I don't know where she is. She's run away to God knows where, and I'm not about to have a party in the middle of a crisis just because Mary's poached a fourteen-pound salmon."

"I keep telling you," Mary's voice was rising. "It's not just the salmon—"

"Whoa. Slow down. Wait a minute." Angel held up

his hand like a traffic cop. "How do we know she ran
away? She could've just gone out, right? Like, for a
little walk, to calm herself? I mean, you guys did have
a fight."

"That's exactly what I said," I said.

Florence shook her head. "She never goes anywhere
by herself. I beg her to go places on her own, but she
never will. She hates going places."

"Okay," Angel said, speaking slowly and calmly.
"Let's be rational about this. We'll go look for her."

"Where?" Her voice got shrill. "Port Authority bus
station? Times Square?" I thought suddenly about this
boy my sister knew who ran away, how they found
him in the Staten Island Ferry terminal, but not for
days, or weeks. How he caught lice, or ringworm,
something gross. My mother said, thank God it wasn't
worse. I didn't think Emily would do something like
that, but how could you be sure?

"Have you called her friends?" he said.

"What friends?" Her laugh was so bitter it made my
throat catch.

"Well, what about the therapist's?" I said. "Couldn't
she have gone there?"

"Oh, please. She hardly knows the man." She
started picking radish scales off the side of the salmon
and cramming them in her mouth. The caterer
flinched.

"What about her father?" Angel said.

"I called Elliott's. That was the first place I tried, but no one answered." The fish now had a big bald patch on one side. "Elliott's still at work, and if she's there, she isn't picking up the phone. I don't want to call him at the office. Elliott blows everything so out of proportion."

Angel gave me a look. He said, "Did she take anything with her?" I had this sudden, absurd image of Emily walking down Central Park West like Huckleberry Finn, her belongings tied up in a handkerchief on a stick. "Did she pack a suitcase? Did she take her wallet? Did you check to see if she took her wallet?"

So we hunted around to see if anything was missing. The apartment looked beautiful. While I was gone, Florence had put flowers in every room, and set out dishes of jelly beans, which looked like little trays of jewels. In the dining room, there was a huge bowl piled with what looked like five hundred dollars worth of fruit. But there was something else different, too. The old scraggly plants, which none of us remembered to water, were gone, replaced by glossy new ones. "Where'd you get the plants?" I said.

"Oh, God," Florence sighed. "On the way home from the shrink. My present to myself." She laughed that harsh laugh again. "It feels like a year ago."

Emily's room looked the way it always did: immaculate. She hated anybody even going in, never mind messing with her things. And here was Florence rummaging through her drawers, yanking out papers, rucking up the perfect piles of perfect, all-white clothes. "Florence! Stop it," I said. "We can see she didn't take anything."

"That's a good sign, right?" Angel said. "She's not, like, moving out."

"I don't know," Florence moaned. "I don't know anything." She suddenly threw herself on Emily's bed and lay there, hugging Emily's stuffed tiger to her chest. "I could kill her," she said into the pillow. "I could just kill her for this."

"Florence?" I said. She was crying again. I touched her shoulder, which I didn't want to do, but I also couldn't just stand there. "Florence, are you okay?" I looked at Angel. He shrugged, but even he looked upset. "Florence, you think this is really serious?" I said. "You really think she ran away? What do you think is going on?"

She didn't answer. I started to ask her again, but just then, she turned over and sat up. Her glasses were askew, so that half of one eye was magnified, the other half normal size. She pulled them off and angrily wiped her eyes. "I'll tell you what I think. I think she's doing this deliberately, to wreck my party. I can see her now, waiting it out, waiting till we're totally hysterical, and then in she'll stroll, all sullen and distant, and disappear into her room and close the door as if nothing's happened, and never even tell me where she's been. And I'll tell you something else," she said. "I'm sick and tired of doing everything in my whole life for her. Let Elliott worry about her tonight. It's time I did something just for me."

"Excuse me?" I said. "Elliott?"

She nodded. "That's where she is, the more I think about it. He's just across town. She has the key."

That didn't sound right to me. "She's never said anything about going there," I said. "What about his threats to put her in the hospital?" I shook my head. "Uh uh. She'd stay away from Elliott."

"Not if it gave her a chance to humiliate me." Queen Florence had returned. "Okay," she said, getting to her feet. "We've got one hour and a million things to do. Sarah, go put on your party dress. Angel's going to help me with the plants. I hate where the florist put that dieffenbachia. I've got to somehow make up with Mary and get myself together. Why are you looking at me like that? You think I don't deserve this party? You think you know more about my daughter than I do?"

What was I going to say? I went and threw on my purple dress, then came out to look for Angel.

"This whole thing really bothers me," I told him. He was in the dining room with Mary, setting up glasses and wine bottles on a folding table. "I mean, I can see Emily waiting it out, that I can see, but not at Elliott's. She'd do something like hide out in the laundry room or, I don't know, the stairwell. I think we should check downstairs and see if we can find her."

"She's a piece of work, that Florence," Mary said. "Unbelievable! Now it's on again! I'm all set to leave and she changes her mind. I should have been a forest ranger."

Angel, meanwhile, was looking me up and down, smiling, saying, "Whoa! You look good." Stretching out the O's, in a way that any other time would have made me totally berserk with happiness.

"I'm getting really worried," I said again.

Just as he started to say something, Florence sidled up. She'd put on pink blush and blue eye shadow, and fixed her hair, and she was wearing this billowy red thing with sort of spirally, woven gold designs, and lots of bracelets and gold earrings as big as hubcaps. "How do I look?" she said, her chin stuck out, like she was daring any of us to say she didn't look spectacular. "Do I look like the birthday girl?"

"Very nice," Mary said.

"You're a fox, Ms. Friedman," Angel said.

She started giving us assignments. I can't even remember what mine was. The minute she walked away, I invented a garbage bag emergency and told Mary I was going to the store. Then I took the service elevator to the basement.

"Emily," I called, peering into the laundry room. Nothing. "Emily!" I checked the room with all the meters. She wasn't there, or in the boiler room, or the repair shop. But I just didn't believe she'd go to Elliott's. I thought of the tree house. It seemed to me she'd go there before she'd go to Elliott's. I tried the lobby. "Did you see Emily Friedman go out earlier?" I asked the doorman.

"People go in and out all day," he said. I asked the elevator man for the other side of the building, and a guy sweeping the floor. They were no help, either.

I was about to head over to the park when I saw a lady coming into the building with this giant cake. Then I saw another bunch of people dressed like Florence, going in with presents. It was seven o'clock. If I didn't go back now, there'd be another Florence freak-out. So I took the service elevator up and used the kitchen door to sneak back into the apartment.

Angel was behind the bar. I told him where I'd been. "Come over here," he said, and he put his arm around me and pulled me close. Which is what I'd longed for, but I couldn't relax into it. "Listen," he said. "You're all upset you didn't find her. But I still think she'll be back. You heard what Florence said. She'll come strollin' in the door."

"What time does it get dark?"

"I don't know—eight-thirty, nine, somewhere in there. Why?"

"What if she's in the park somewhere and it gets dark?"

"What would she be doing in the park?" he said. "She's a smart kid. She'll be back. You'll see."

Now all the guests were streaming in, these dressed-up, smiling, middle-aged people, shouting out hellos and handing Florence presents. I tried to stay with Angel at the bar, but Florence called me over next to her, and literally held me there beside her. Everyone was milling around, kissing everyone else—the kind of kisses where they stick their faces at you and go "*mwa*," half an inch away. People looking me over, saying things like, "And who is this *delightful* young lady?" and "So this is Sarah? I've heard so *much* about you!"

I so badly wanted to believe Angel that at first, each time the door opened, I kept thinking it was Emily, but after forty or fifty people had come in and handed Florence presents, and Florence had said, forty or fifty times, "Oh really, you *shouldn't!*" I knew that he was wrong. She wasn't coming back.

And now the place was filling up. Mary and Ruth were smiling, carrying around trays of minipizzas. Every time I glanced at Angel, he was smiling, pouring somebody a drink, looking cute and charming, like a bartender in a movie. Florence's smile looked like it was welded on. I was the only one not smiling.

Two couples arrived with girls Emily's age. "Where's Emily?" one of the girls asked, as Florence *mwa*-ed the parents. I kept staring at the girl's green braces. I didn't know how to answer.

Florence, though, smooth as can be, said, "I'm sorry, Amanda, unfortunately, Emily couldn't be here. She and her father had special plans."

"What a shame," one of the mothers said.

"But on your birthday?" Another lady in a black jumpsuit joined the conversation.

"So is she living with her father these days?" the first lady said. "We haven't seen Emily in ages."

"How *is* Emily? Is she okay?"

"Certainly she's okay," Florence said. "She's fine." Her mouth was still smiling, but something about her eyes made me grab her arm and pull her toward the kitchen.

"It's getting late," I said. "If Emily's at Elliott's, wouldn't he have called by now?"

"Not if they're having too good a time trading Evil Florence stories," she said. "I'll call him in a minute. I haven't even said hello to everybody."

"But it's going to be dark soon," I said.

Florence glared. "I said I'd call him in a minute." I followed her to the living room. Even with the air conditioner, it was hot in there—hot, noisy, and filled with the smells of alcohol, cigarette smoke, flowers, and perfume. A man with a big nose and a teensy little chin barreled over and kissed Florence on the mouth. He leaned so close to me, I was scared he was going to kiss me, too, but he just waggled his eyebrows and said, "Are you only a mother's helper, or do you help fathers too?"

"Oh, Mort!" Florence giggled. "You're impossible." So this was Morty, her accountant, the one she'd had the dream about. I couldn't bear the way he kept smiling at me, but I couldn't leave before she said what she was going to do, so I stood there, breathing in Mort's cigarette fumes, listening to him blather on about his golf game, watching Florence smiling in his face and telling him, too, that it was Emily's night out with her dad.

When a lady walked over to me and said, "Dear, would you mind terribly going over to the bar and getting me a glass of chardonnay?" I pushed my way through the crowd to Angel.

"It's eight o'clock at night," I said. "She's not coming back."

"So what do you want to do?" he said.

"Call Elliott myself," I said. "If she's not there, we're going out to find her."

CHAPTER 17

I called Elliott. He was there, but Emily wasn't. "What do you mean, missing?" he demanded. "Where were you? Where was her mother? Who's in charge there? Anyone? Is anyone there looking out for Emily?" I didn't realize how hard I'd been hoping he'd sound nice, so I could tell him everything and he would handle it. "Where's Florence," he demanded. "No, wait, don't get her. I'm coming right over." I tried to head him off, but he had hung up.

I was telling Angel all this when Florence walked in, carrying a drink. "Oho!" she said, looking at Angel sitting on my bed. "So that's where you two are." She was smiling this tight, unpleasant smile. "We were all wondering." She put her hand on Angel's shoulder.

"Angel, darling, she is adorable, no question, but (a) isn't she a trifle young? and (b) I absolutely need you at the bar. I'm paying you to work, not mess around with Sarah. You understand that." He nodded.

"But we've got to go find Emily," I said.

"There's a whole line of people waiting for their drinks," Florence said.

Angel looked right at her and nodded and let her steer him out the door.

I couldn't believe it. I stuffed some money in my pocket and went after them. "Where are you going?" I called to Angel. He turned and gave me a helpless smile and muttered something about working, and I was suddenly so angry it took all my willpower not to cry. "Mess around?" I said. "She thinks we're messing around? You tell her, Angel. We're in here calling *her* husband about *her* missing daughter while she's having a birthday party." I wasn't shouting, but my words were loud enough for Florence to hear. She immediately glanced around to see if anyone was listening. "You're the one flirting with your accountant, Florence, ignoring what's going on. You're the one pretending everything's fine, doing nothing to find her." We'd reached the living room now, but I didn't care who heard me. "This is an emergency!" I shouted. "It's going to be dark soon and your daughter's missing."

"You're hysterical," Florence said.

"Don't tell me what I am," I said. "You don't know what I am. That's exactly what you do with Emily. You're always telling her how she is and how she feels. You don't know how she feels. You don't even know where she is. Where she is, is off somewhere hiding to get away from you."

Her eyes goggled. "How dare you!" She puffed herself up like a pigeon. "This is not my fault." But just as suddenly, she deflated. "You didn't really call Elliott?" I nodded. "And she wasn't there?" I could see her trying to hang on to her control.

"No. And now he's coming over here, so you'd better do something fast."

"Oh, God!" She took a big gulp of her drink. "Now you're getting me hysterical. What am I going to do?"

"Flo, dear, is there some trouble with Emily?" A lady came over and put her hand on Florence's arm. "Is everything all right?"

"Everything's fine," Florence said, quickly finishing the drink. "Just fine." She turned to Angel. "Angel, darling, go with Elaine over to the bar and fix us both a nice big margarita."

"You're going to just walk away?" I called to Angel, as he and the lady started toward the dining room. "You're not going to help me either?"

I was crying by the time I'd run down the backstairs

to the lobby. What if Emily wasn't where I thought she was? What if I couldn't find her? It wasn't dark yet, but it was getting there. As I ran across the street, a carful of guys stopped at the light and called things at me. Why hadn't I changed out of the purple dress? I started toward the park. There were lots of people on the street, and it felt like they were all looking at me. Even some guy rummaging through a garbage can called out, "Smile!" as I went by. I walked faster. There were guys lounging against the wall, sitting on the benches, drinking beer, blasting music from their boom boxes. "Hey, sweet thing!" "Hey, baby, slow down. What's the rush?"

At last, I reached the road that led up into the park. The park looked huge and murky, full of hiding places. In one of the trees, something white and wispy flapped its wings. It looked more like a ghost than any bird I'd seen. Or maybe it was a bat. I felt a warning tingling in my fingertips. My whole life, I'd heard how dangerous it was in Central Park. Whatever you do, don't ever go there after dark. And it was dark there now, under all the trees, much darker than the street.

I checked around, then started up the winding road, staying in the middle, in case someone was lurking in the bushes. A man ran past me with his dog. You're fine, I told myself. Now I could see that the bat was just a shredded plastic shopping bag, caught among the branches. You'll go get Emily and bring her back, and you'll be fine. But then I heard a strange muttering, and a clanking, clattering sound behind me. A man in a hooded sweatshirt and a raggedy winter coat mumbled and cursed as he labored up the hill, pushing a baby stroller loaded down with bags of cans and bottles. My heart was thumping. I started running. When I got to where the road turned, I hid behind a tree and held my breath until he passed my hiding place. "Please," I prayed, "don't let him stop at the playground."

When he'd clanked off, still talking to himself, I raced across the grass to the playground, and peered through the gate. It looked deserted: no kids, no carriages, no lovers. The wooden climbing pyramid loomed spookily. The framework for the tire swing towered against the sky like a gallows. My nerves were tuned up so high, I could hear everything: insects thrumming, the roar of traffic on the park drive.

"Emily!" I called softly, "are you in here?" There was no answer.

I tiptoed in, keeping an eye on the open gate, half expecting it to snap shut, trapping me inside. This playground looked much bigger than I remembered. To get to the tree house, which was practically at the back fence, you had to cross this wooden boardwalk straight across the center—which was totally exposed.

I felt the panic rising in my throat, the sweat trickling down inside my dress.

I forced myself to breathe, counted to three, then ran like hell for the tree house. I climbed the ladder. She wasn't on the first level. She wouldn't be, though. It was the top she liked. That top room was her secret hiding place. But what if someone else was there, instead? What if he'd been watching me this whole time, and was just waiting for me to climb into his lair?

But she was there, huddled in the far corner, her arms clasped around her knees.

"Thank God!" I said, as I hauled myself onto the platform. "I thought I'd never make it." Emily looked at me, but didn't say anything. I slumped down across from her and leaned against the wall. "I was so scared," I said. I wiped my face on my skirt, then I started telling her about the party, how Florence thought she was at Elliott's, how I'd narrowly escaped a crazy man, on and on, babbling. She still hadn't said a word. She just sat there, staring into space. And suddenly, I was so mad I literally saw spots. "Don't thank me or anything," I said. "Don't act like a normal human being and be grateful that I risked my life to come and get you. Plus called your delightful father and told your mother what I think of her, which really pissed her off. Plus had a horrendous day worrying about you."

"I've been here all afternoon," Emily said.

"What's that supposed to mean?"

She picked at her knee. "I've just been sitting here. Waiting."

"Oh great," I yelled. "That's really great. And I'm supposed to know and come and get you. You could've said so. You could've written me a note. Or sent a fax. Or hired a skywriter. Yo! Sarah! I'm running away. Come and save me. How was I supposed to know? And how'd I get this job? Who elected me? I'm not even related to you." She was crying now, but not regular out-loud boohoos—these whimpery sniffs that made me even madder. "You don't even cry right. Sniffling like I did something to you, when you're the one who ran away. Shit, if you're going to cry, at least have the guts to make some noise!"

"You hate me," she said. "What'd you even come here for?"

" 'Cause I thought I was your friend."

"You don't know what my life is like. You don't know anything about me."

"Whose fault is that?" I said.

"You don't know what it's like to have problems." She was still whimpering. "Everything's so easy for you. You're so thin and pretty. . . ."

"Earth to Emily," I called. "Reality check." Another of my father's truly obnoxious expressions. I'll never know why, in times of stress, I always come out sounding like my father. "This is me, Sarah, you're talking to."

"You are. Compared to me, you are. And you've got this great family who's not crazy, and friends, and—"

"I told you. You're my friend."

"And you always seem so . . . ," she struggled for the word, "comfortable."

"Not now I'm not." I looked out over the park, at the last few runners and bikers heading home. "Emily, all the normal people are leaving. Can we just get out of here? I just want to make it out alive."

"You never gain weight and everything you do comes out right and you always know what to say. . . ."

I started to tell her she was crazy, but then I thought about it. "I guess I did know what to say to Florence. I said to her the same thing you just said to me. I told her she doesn't know you."

She stopped picking at her knee. "What'd she say?"

"Nothing. I didn't give her a chance. I told her she doesn't know the first thing about you. I told her she doesn't see you at all. She's never seen you. She just sees herself. She goes on and on about how Emily's so good and so perfect, and that's fine, as long as you're what she wants, which is that you have to be just like her—a total Florence clone—or if you're not like her, then you have to be Her Creation. It's that or else you're nothing. She's a total bully, but in this sneaky way, where you're never sure. She like, gets you confused, like how she wants you to eat but she's obsessed with being fat. And she does it in this way that you don't even know you're confused, till your head's spinning and you don't know what you think."

Some of that was what I'd said to Florence, but some of it was things I wished I'd said, things I'd just thought of now. I wasn't even sure all of it was about Emily.

Anyway, I guess I said too much. Because at one end of the platform, there was this chain link bridge which looked about ten feet long and led to a farther platform, and while I was talking, Emily stood up, grabbed the chain railing and began to walk across. The bridge swung and teetered with every step. "Come back here, Emily," I called. I don't even like crossing bridges in the car, never mind walking across wobbly chain ones in the dark. "We have to get out of here." She wasn't that far away, but I could hardly see her.

"No," she said, "I'm not leaving."

"Emily," I said.

"She'll be glad I'm gone. And now you've said those things, so you can't go back either."

"We can go back," I said. "Of course we can go back." Looking out over the side, I thought I saw a police scooter circling the playground, on the path. I wanted to yell to him, but I knew he wouldn't hear. "So what if she's mad. We're mad at her, too. You could even tell her . . ."

"I want to stay here." Her voice rose. "No one'll bother us here. It's not cold or anything. And there are no bugs. In the morning, we can like, bring stuff up here, food and stuff, and nobody will know. It's nice here. Please can we, Sarah? Please?"

"We can't stay here." I was wishing that the policeman would come back. I was imagining crazy people with baby strollers all converging on the playground. I looked at my wrist. "I don't even know what time it is. I can't even see my watch."

"This is my secret place. It's always been my secret place. It's the only place I'm safe." I knew it was after nine, because there were cars again on the park drive. "If we stay here, I promise you I'll eat. I'll eat anything you say. I'll prove it. Go out and get something . . . anything, and bring it back and I'll eat all of it right now."

Those words had a horribly familiar ring. It's what she'd said when Florence took the bike. "I can't deal with this," I said.

"You're the only person in the world who cares about me."

"Don't do this to me, Emily." I put my foot down on the bridge. It swayed sickeningly. Why had I thought that I could deal with Emily alone? I gripped the railing and tentatively took a step. Just don't look down, I told myself.

"I don't care . . . ," Emily began.

"Would you shut up!" I said, teeth clenched. Two more steps to go.

"You can leave," she said, as I stepped onto the platform. "I don't blame you. I'm disgusting, and now I've gotten you in trouble. . . ."

"I am not leaving you, not after I just crossed the stupid bridge. So just shut up." I took her by the arm.

"Ow!" she said. I didn't let go. "What are you do-ing?" I started for the ladder. "Where are you taking me?"

I scanned the playground as well as I could in the dark. It seemed empty. "Just be careful going down," I said. At the bottom, I felt my pocket to make sure my money was still there, then peered around again and grabbed her hand. "Run!"

She was crying now. "I can't go home," she sobbed as I dragged her, stumbling and resisting, to the gate. Out the gate we ran, across the grass, and over to the road. "You're not taking me home!"

"Just shut up, Emily, and trust me!" I said, running faster, down the curving road. And now we were at the street. "We're not going to your house," I said, struggling to catch my breath. "We're going to my house. I'm taking you home with me."

CHAPTER 18

And that's what we did—walked to the subway, then rode down to Penn Station and waited for a train. It was a long wait. Emily paced up and down in the waiting room. She drummed her fingers, picked at her knee, worried out loud that Florence would be waiting at my house, or that Elliott would show up there, even though I hadn't told anyone what we were doing.

My house was dark when the taxi dropped us off: no lights on, even in my sister's room. It was well past midnight. I didn't have my keys. In the moonlight, my rhododendron bush looked shorter than I remembered. Shorter and flatter. "Why are we just standing here?" Emily said after a while. "Shouldn't we ring the bell or something?"

"Don't rush me," I said. "I don't know how it's going to be, being in the same house with all of them again."

"You think they'll yell at you? When they see I'm here?"

"No, no." I shook my head. "That's not their style, to yell. They're too refined. Remember the famous Bad Dog Treatment? I told you about that, right? There's Richard and Barbara, and the lovely Shelley, and then there's good old Bowser."

"Sa-rah!" Emily clearly didn't think much of that.

"You're the only one I'd ever tell that to, you know." It was so much easier not to hate them when I was at the Friedmans. "Your house may be bizarre, but I like the way I am there. I like it so much better than how I was at home. And what if I like, instantaneously revert? What if I don't even know it?"

"Stop it, Sarah," she said. "You hate it when I put myself down."

"Okay," I said. "But if I say anything that seems Bowser-like to you, will you please give me a kick or something?"

I rang, but we had to wait so long, I told Emily maybe they'd gone away, like on vacation, and not told me. But then the foyer light snapped on and there was Dad, in his pajamas, staring at me as if I'd landed from another planet. "Sarah! It's the middle of the night!" I knew he'd say that. This man goes to bed at twenty-five past ten every night of his life. You could wake him up at quarter of eleven and he'd say it was the middle of the night. "Barbara!" he yelled. "Barb! Come down. It's Sarah. What's happened?" he said to me. "What are you doing here?"

"You pruned my rhododendron," I said.

He nodded. "Bob Horner came a couple of weeks ago. I had him trim all the shrubbery. The damn bushes were blocking all the light." He patted down his hair. "How in God's name did you get here?"

"Train," I said. "The rhododendron looks so flat." My father looked from me to Emily, waiting for me to say something. In the glare of the outside light, Emily looked truly terrible: her eyes were glittery and watchful, but they had huge hollows under them and everything about her, from her hair down to her socks, was sagging. "Emily sort of needed to get away," I said.

"In the middle of the night?" my father said.

"Sarah! What are you doing here? Are you okay?" My mother hurried to the doorway, tying her robe as she came.

"They took the train," my father said.

"Is she in some sort of trouble?" my mother said.

"How come everyone assumes . . . ," I said, but

Emily looked at me and I stopped myself. "No, I'm not in any trouble. I'm fine."

"What's going on?" It was my sister, Shelley. "Sarah. Cool dress," she said. She'd clearly been asleep but she looked as immaculately groomed as always. "Who's this?"

"Emily," I said. "This is Emily."

"Why didn't you call?" my mother said. "You should have told us you were coming home."

Emily looked at me and evidently decided I needed help. I could see her pull herself together. "Please don't be mad at Sarah," she said. "This is my fault. I wouldn't let her call." She took a deep breath and blew it out. "I left."

"Left where?" Dad said.

"Left the apartment."

"Left, as in ran away?"

She nodded. "And Sarah had to come and find me in the park. . . ."

"Central Park?" Shelley's eyes were wide. "Weren't you scared?"

Emily nodded. "But I didn't want to go home. I can't go home."

"Can we please go inside," I said.

So we went into the kitchen. It was so weird being back here after all this time. I'd forgotten how completely bland and spotless this house was. I felt as if I'd stepped into a floor wax ad. Or one of those dreams where one part of you is the main character, while at the same time some other part is hovering up there near the ceiling, wondering who all these people are. I mean, picture it: my father firing off a thousand questions, not waiting for the answers; my mother asking a million other questions, while she makes a pot of coffee, saying, as she always says, that she can't think straight till she's had some coffee; Emily picking at her nails, her eyes darting from my father to my mother, not knowing which question to answer first; me, wandering from sink to fridge to table, my brain still too revved up for me to sit; and my sister, who has always known what was important in life, asking me where I got the dress.

Then, she noticed my earrings. "I don't believe this!" she said, coming over and pushing back my hair. "Sarah actually got her ears pierced after she told us she would never in a million years even consider. . . . God, Sarah, it looks really nice. This is, like, a whole new you."

"Good thing, huh?" I said. "Anything's an improvement, right?"

"*Woof*," Emily said, under her breath.

"I beg your pardon?" my mother said.

"I coughed," Emily said. "I have a cough."

"I can't believe it," Shelley said again. "You look so great."

This time, Emily *woofed* before I could say anything.

Then my mother called Florence. She wanted Emily to do it, but Emily said, "You don't know Florence. If I talk to Florence, I'll end up going back there. Sarah promised me I wouldn't have to go back there." Which I hadn't, but I was not about to contradict her.

So my mother told Florence where we were and how I'd found Emily and brought her here. Then there was this extremely long time when all she said was "Oh, dear," and "You're kidding," and "I had no idea," frowning, glancing over at Emily, then at me, then back to Emily. Shelley got bored and went to bed.

"I don't want to talk to her," Emily said again. "I hope she doesn't make me talk to her."

"Tell her not to come," I said. "She'll want to come and get Emily."

"Girls! *Shhh!*" my father said.

"Please, don't let her come," Emily said.

"Tell her again, she's fine," I said. "Make sure she understands that we're both fine."

Then my mother held the phone out and said, "Emily, your father wants to talk to you."

I can't describe the feelings that flashed across Emily's face. "Elliott?" she said. My mother nodded.

"Daddy's with my mother? Are you sure? He's at my apartment?"

My mother nodded again. "He wants to speak to you."

"That can't be," Emily said. "He hasn't been there in a year. He used to come on weekends, to pick me up, but he always waited in the lobby. He wouldn't even talk to Florence."

My mother put her hand over the receiver. "Well, he's there now," she said, "and he really wants to talk to you. Just a minute," she said into the phone. I could see her trying to figure out whose side she was on.

"I don't know what to say to him." Emily looked panicky. "Does he sound angry, or nice?" I remembered how he'd sounded on the phone with me, which was definitely not nice.

"He sounds really concerned about you," my mother said. "He sounds as if he loves you."

Emily put her hands to her mouth. She looked about to cry. Which made me feel like crying, too. Even my father looked emotional. Then suddenly, she stood up and ran out of the room. I got up to follow, worried she might run away again. My father got up too. "Oh, no," my mother sighed. But into the phone, she said, "Mr. Friedman, Elliott, I'll tell you the truth. Emily looks like she needs a little time to think things through. She's had a tough day. Maybe we should let her get some sleep and call you in the morning."

Emily hadn't run away. We found her in the living room, curled up in my father's chair. And she was sound asleep. "Why didn't you tell us all this was going on?" my father whispered. My mother had come in, too, and they were both looking at me really sternly. "Why didn't you tell us what kind of situation you were in? Why didn't you come home earlier and talk to us?"

"I didn't need to. I was handling it," I said. "I was helping."

"What about the anorexia?" my mother said. "Look at her. This girl has a serious problem. She's starving. How could you not tell us?"

"She's working on it," I said. "We got her a therapist. We're all working on it. . . ."

"I had no idea this is what you were getting into."

"You didn't tell us any of it," my father said.

"You'd just have gotten all upset and told me to come home."

"And we'd have been right, too," he said. "This is not a normal home situation you were in."

"Can't you understand?" I got up and went over and stood looking out the window, so they couldn't see my face. It was completely black outside. "I like it there.

It's interesting to me." I searched for a way to explain it to them. "They like me very much. They think I'm great."

"You are great," my mother said, but that didn't register till later.

I turned toward them. "Plus I'm, like, her last hope. Emily even told me that's why Florence hired me. She's got no friends. I like Florence, but she's a lunatic. And Elliott's been threatening to put Emily in the hospital if she doesn't gain weight soon. I know you think I can't do anything." In my head, Emily's voice *woofed* loudly. "But I am helping. It's hard to tell, sometimes, but I'm helping both of them."

"We should have called more, kept better track," my father said. "I thought a few times about calling you, but your mother said, give you room."

"You were always like that," my mother said. "You went your own way, even as a little girl. They always say second children are supposed to be the easy ones, but . . ."

"Would you spare me, please? I don't want to hear about the sandbox," I said. I thought that might wake Emily, but she didn't stir.

"No, remember, Rich, how she would never sit in her stroller? Shelley loved the stroller. I had to pry Shelley out of the stroller. And even now, when something's troubling Shelley, Shelley always comes to me."

"And me," my father said. "She comes to me."

"I'm not Shelley, okay?" I said. "I'm sorry. I'm just not the cuddly type. Emily can accept that, even if you can't."

"Oh, Sarah." My mother came over and looked at me and shook her head. "I'm sorry this is working out this way. But I'm glad to see you."

"Don't think we're not very proud of you for what you did," my father said. "You did the right thing, trying to help this girl."

My mother said, "What I want to say is, you and I are not that great at talking to each other. I wish it didn't have to be so hard. What could happen if you came to me once in a while and said, 'Mom, I could use a little help?' I'd like to help you." Then she put her arms around me.

The tiny part of me that was still up there near the ceiling thought: Mom? I don't call her Mom. I've never called her Mom. The other part said, into her shoulder, "Damn it!" Because I was crying. Which I never do in front of anyone. Particularly my parents. "I need a tissue," I said. I went over and got one and blew my nose. "I really want to help her," I said. "I don't know why I want to so much. A lot of the time I don't even like her. . . ."

"Families are like that," my mother said.

I blew my nose again. "So what are we going to do?"

My mother shook her head. "I don't know. It looks like Emily's mother is going to show up first thing in the morning. We'll have to talk to Emily and figure something out. But right now, we need to go to bed." She called Emily's name till Emily's eyes opened. Then she took her arm and helped her up, and without saying anything, we all went upstairs.

I gave Emily my white nightgown and put her in my extra bed, the one my parents had bought for all the sleepovers I was supposed to have. I wanted to make a list of things I needed to think about, but before I could start, my eyes began to close.

I can't tell you how Emily slept, but I slept better, that night, than I'd slept in weeks.

CHAPTER 19

"Sarah, wake up! Don't let my mother in here. I don't want her here!"

It was seven-thirty the next morning, and I was in the middle of a dream. Angel was about to kiss me. It was dark, and we were in my yard and he felt really bad he hadn't gone with me to look for Emily. "I really like you," he was saying. "My whole life, I never met a girl like you." You can't just end a dream when someone tells you that, even if you are still pissed at him. So even as I felt Emily poke me and heard my mother's voice, urging, "Really, why don't you just wait downstairs . . . ," Dream Angel continued to stroke his thumb across my palm. "Don't be mad with me," he said. "See, I even brought the lady from the fish store. She brought your mom this fish." I suddenly noticed there was a gigantic mackerel on the grass.

But the fish store lady sounded just like Florence, and her voice was getting closer. "You'll have to excuse the way I look," I heard her say. "I didn't get one minute's sleep. And when Elliott called at six and said he'd called a cab and would be by in fifteen minutes, I just threw on some clothes—you wouldn't believe the way I left the house—and there was almost no traffic. . . . Oh, God, Emily!"

I opened my eyes as Florence burst into my room. She rushed toward Emily, grabbing her before Emily could run out, and hugged her so hard it looked like she was squashing her. Emily's whole body stiffened instantly. And then I saw Elliott. He looked nothing like what I'd been imagining. For one thing, he was very short. Something about the way he strode into the room made me think of Mighty Mouse, that cartoon mouse who sings, "Here I come to save the day." I hated him immediately. I hated the way his jeans were starched and his T-shirt was ironed and tucked in. I hated the way he came over to my bed before he'd even hugged Emily, and cleared his throat and said, "Elliott Friedman. Emily's father. You must be Sarah," and made me shake his clammy hand. And when he did go over to hug Emily, I hated the way I could see hope flare up in her eyes, then turn immediately to fear.

When he let her go, Emily got back in bed and pulled the covers up and pressed herself against the wall. And then there was this silence. Nobody, not even Florence, said anything. I don't know what Elliott and Florence had been hoping for—some glorious reunion, probably, some touchy-feely Forgiveness Fest. Whatever it was, it was not this interminable, edgy silence.

My parents, still in their bathrobes, had been standing in the hall, watching all this carefully. Just when I thought we were all going to explode, they came in, and my mother put her hand on Florence's shoulder. "Listen, Mrs. Friedman," she said, "it was a long, hard night. Come on downstairs with us. She'll have a shower and pull herself together. . . ."

Florence shrugged her hand off. "I waited all night to see her."

My parents looked at each other. "In that case, Sarah and Richard and I will leave you three to talk," my mother said.

"No! Don't leave me!" Emily's voice was shrill.

"Actually," Elliott cleared his throat again, "we left the cab waiting outside. Emily, we've put these nice people out more than enough already. Now it's time to go." He turned to my parents. "You've been most understanding with us."

"I'm not going," Emily said.

"Of course you are," he said, trying hard to smile. "Now I want you to get up and put your clothes on and get ready."

"I can't," she said. "I'll hide. I'll run away again. I really will."

"Now Emily, I'm going to be straight with you." He jingled the change in his pants pocket. "I'm in no mood for a hard time. Not after what you've put your mother and me through. We've let you get away with too much nonsense already." He cleared his throat again. "It's time to lay down the law."

Florence groaned. "Oh, give us a break, Elliott. You always say that. You're full of these big threats, but when it comes down to it, where are you?"

"I don't see you making her eat," he said to Florence. "I don't see you exactly taking charge." And the fight was on. Elliott was clearly one of those guys who are more comfortable being angry than upset. When in doubt, get mad. And we already know about Florence. I was desperate for the bathroom, but I could not see leaving Emily alone with them.

They had nothing in common, to look at them: Florence was big and Elliott was short; he was as neat as Emily, and she was a mess; she waved her arms and yelled while he got tighter and more fidgety. But from the first "Calm down!" "No, you calm down!" their fighting style meshed perfectly. First Elliott threatened Emily and warned of dire consequences, while Florence begged her and tried to bribe her and blamed herself. Then they switched off, and Elliott cajoled while Florence became the blusterer. And while the battle raged around her—each accusing the other of not knowing how to handle Emily; of standing idly by while she starved herself to death; of being a wretched, useless, lousy, crazy, failure of a parent—while they paced and hovered and shook their fingers at her, Emily just lay there, totally inert, not saying anything. Except once, when Florence, during the guilt phase, said, "I'm disappointed in you, Emily," and Emily said, so softly Florence had to ask her twice to repeat it, "You should be used to that by now." And one other time, Elliott, back in macho mode, said, "I brought you into the world young lady . . . ," and she answered, "and then you left me alone with *her*."

That's when I really looked at Emily carefully and realized something. I mean, Florence looked at least ten years older than she did the day before. Elliott looked like if he didn't cry, he'd burst. But Emily's eyes were bright, and I don't mean with tears. I suddenly remembered what I'd figured out with Angel: this was a power thing. And Emily had all the power.

Here I'd been thinking, poor Emily, bullied by these awful people, cowering in the bed. But these people were scared out of their minds. Emily had them totally tied in knots.

"I have to say something!" I said. I jumped up out of bed. They stopped arguing and stared at me. My parents' eyes widened. I wished I were wearing more than the ratty pajamas I'd pulled out of the drawer at three o'clock in the morning, when we went to bed, but so it went. "You're going round and round and everyone's just getting more upset. I can tell you've said these things a thousand times. You know your lines by heart. Meanwhile, Emily's lying there, and we're all acting like poor little helpless Emily, she's dying, but I happen to know she isn't going to die. She doesn't want to die."

"Then why won't she eat?" Elliott said. "She will die, if she doesn't eat."

Emily was looking at me so intensely I wanted to say something really brilliant, something so right nobody could ignore it. Something that would solve this whole thing for them. "All I know is, this is not about food. She'd eat if she could, if other things felt okay. It's like, if you can't control anything else in your life, you can at least control what you put in your mouth. Excuse me, Emily, if what I'm going to say pisses you off. Just look at her, lying there like the Queen of the

Bedroom. It's not like she can't control anything. She's got you guys jumping around like dancing dogs. She wasn't helpless when she ran to Central Park. She wasn't helpless last night, when she helped me with my parents." Out of the corner of my eye, I saw my parents nodding. "That's why I know she can be all right." I stopped to catch my breath, then added, "I think you guys should go home."

That, evidently, felt like pushing it, to my father. "Sarah . . . ," he said. "I think you should stay out of this."

But Elliott held up his hand. "Let Sarah talk."

"I'm not saying it to be rude," I said. "I know how worried you are about her. You had to come. But I happen to know she's trying to get better. I mean, look at her. This girl is tough, or she'd have caved in and eaten long ago."

"Can I say something?" Emily said. She took a deep breath. "You're all talking about me, saying how sick I am, how tough I am. But you don't ask me how I feel."

"So tell us," Florence said. "We're waiting for you to tell us." She said it in this belligerent way that I thought would shut Emily up. But Emily sat up in the bed and clutched the pillow to her chest.

"Everything is wrong," she said. "My whole life is wrong. But it's not like that here. I'm happy here. . . ."

"You've been here for what?" Florence said. "Eight hours? Not even, and most of it you were asleep."

"I don't care. I like it here. I'm safe here."

Florence started to protest but Elliott shut her up. "You don't feel safe at home?" he said.

She shook her head but didn't look at them. "At home I feel like . . . I don't know . . . like . . . like there's someone sitting on me so I can't breathe."

"I'm keeping you from breathing?" Florence said. "I'm suffocating you? That's what you're saying?" She flung her arms out and made this sort of moaning sob. "That's the last thing I meant to do. That's what my parents did to me. That's why I've always tried to encourage you to be yourself, to do anything you want—"

"Florence," I said.

"Florence, she's trying to talk to you," Elliott said. "To us. You have to try to listen. You can see it's hard for her."

"For her?" Florence said. "How do you think it is for me, hearing I'm suffocating my own daughter?"

"Shut up, Florence," Elliott said. "For once, can you just shut up."

"You're the lawyer. You interrupt as much as I do."

"Can we not do this?" Elliott said. "Do you think it's possible? Because I think Sarah's right."

"I know she's right," Florence said. "You think I

don't know she's right? She was right yesterday too, when she gave me such hell at the party." My parents gave me a questioning look but didn't say anything. "You think that doesn't make all this infinitely worse?"

Elliott walked over to Emily's bed and sat down next to her. "As long as we're all telling the truth," he said, "can I tell you the truth, Emily?" She nodded. "I felt very nervous about seeing you. I told myself, Here's your chance. Here's your chance to make things right, but I was afraid I'd come here and everything would be the same. I want things to be different with all of us, but I don't know how to do it. I'm at my wit's end, Emily. I don't know what to do."

"That's why I want to stay here," Emily said. "Here I can be someone else. At home . . ."

He put his hand on her shoulder. "I don't want you to be someone else," he said. "I want you to be Emily, only happy again, the way you used to be. I wish it could all be the way it used to be."

Florence was crying now. "We were on the phone for an hour last night with Dr. Kahn. . . ."

"Who, incidentally, is a smart man," Elliott said to Florence. "You should try to listen to him. . . ."

"Daddy? When you said home, before?" Emily said. "When you wanted to take me home?" The sentence trailed off, but I could hear the expectation in her voice, the wariness. I looked at Florence.

"What are you asking?" Elliott said. He started jingling his change so hard I was afraid it would spontaneously combust.

"I don't know. I guess, like, who's going to be there?"

"You, for one. And your mother. And Sarah, if she hasn't had enough of us."

Emily was twisting up the corner of her pillow. "What about you?" she said to Elliott. Her voice was very small. "Will you be there?"

"I'll come there," he said. "To see you. I'd like to see you often. If that's what you want."

"I thought maybe . . ." She wrung the fabric tighter.

He shook his head. "Your mother and I . . . I really can't come back to live."

Emily began to cry. She didn't even hide her face, just looked at him with the tears running down, and her face all crumpled up and shouted, "I'm sorry. I'm sorry. How many times do I have to say I'm sorry. I didn't mean to make you leave."

"Emily." Elliott put his arms around her. "You didn't make me leave."

"You say that, but I know—"

"You don't know." He sounded like somebody had their hands around his neck. "If you think that, you're just wrong. It had nothing to do with you. My feelings about you never changed."

"Then how could you leave me? How could you want to dump me in some hospital?"

"I didn't leave you. I didn't want to leave you. And I'd never dump you anywhere. I said that because I was so worried. And I didn't know what to do. You have to help me, Emily. Help me help you. Work with me. Work with us. We want to, Emily. But we're not good at this."

"You stink at this." She wiped her eyes with her arm. "And I'm not going back now."

My father stepped closer. "May I make a suggestion?" he said. "Why can't she stay here for the weekend? We've hardly even seen Sarah yet. And it'll be no problem, having Emily."

"She doesn't eat a lot," I said. Florence and Elliott ignored that. They were looking at each other. But my mother almost smiled.

"She could stay here till Sunday night," my father said.

"Yes," Emily said, nodding.

"I don't know," Florence said. "She has an appointment with Dr. Kahn at nine Monday morning."

"We'll drive her back," my mother said. "We'll drive them both back, depending on what Sarah wants.

What *are* your plans, Sarah? We haven't talked about that."

"I'm going back," I said. "I'm her friend."

"Sounds like that's settled," my father said. "We'll drive in Sunday night."

"I don't know," Florence said. "I just hope she eats."

"Florence," my mother said, "she'll be fine. You heard what Sarah said. Now, these girls haven't even brushed their teeth. So we'll go downstairs and we'll make you a nice breakfast and then, when the girls are ready to come down, if you want to talk some more, we can discuss it over breakfast."

"Hallelujah!" I said when my parents finally got them out of there. I went immediately to the bathroom. When I got back, Emily was making her bed. "So, are you mad at me?" I said. "For what I said about you?" She shook her head. She pulled the bedspread off and began smoothing out the sheets. "I thought I was pretty good," I said. "But your father was pretty good too. Considering that I wanted to kill him when he came in here. And did you hear *my* father?" I dropped my voice an octave. " 'Sounds like that's settled.' " Emily pulled up the blanket and stretched the top sheet over it and tucked the whole thing in. That bed had never been so neat. "It was pretty amazing, don't you think? I mean, we told them, and even old Flo was listening. I'm telling you, things are going to be different, Emily." I felt, suddenly, like I was going to overflow with happiness. "You know what else is wonderful," I said. "Being back in my own room with my own messes that I made myself. See this . . ." I pointed to the shelves with my feather collection and my piles of fossil rocks and seashells and my giant wasp nest. "My mother hates this stuff. I was so sure I'd come back and find she'd chucked it all." I pointed out my cello case propped in the corner. "I bet you never even knew I played the cello." I stuck a blue jay feather in my hair and struck a pose. "Whattaya think?"

But Emily had gone over to the mirror on the closet door and was looking at herself. She sucked in her stomach, turned this way and that, and studied herself from different angles, frowning.

"What are you doing?" I said.

She moved over to my dresser and checked herself in that mirror, then went back to the first. "This is so weird," she said. She sounded really confused. "Come over here and look. There's something about the mirrors in your house. For some reason, I don't look quite as fat here as I look at home."

The way I felt then went beyond happy, to giddy, euphoric, delirious. First I hugged her. Then I got this sudden, uncontrollable urge to show her all my poems.

I must have been delirious. No one had seen my poems since the Great Artichoke Fiasco. I handed her the folder, then lay down on my bed and closed my eyes and told myself I was resting. I kept them shut as long as I could, but when I sneaked a look at her, she was pacing around the room. She'd read a little, then go back to the mirror and stare at herself again. Read another, then stand in front of my dresser, looking at herself. "Aren't you going to say anything?" I said.

"I'm thinking," she said.

My throat started to get that closed-up feeling. "It's okay if you hate them," I said. "I wrote most of them a long time ago, anyway."

"Sarah! *Woof!* Remember?"

"Hey." I tried to sound nonchalant. "What can you expect from a girl who compares herself to vegetables. . . ."

"Stop that. *Arf!*" she said.

"Someone whose best friend was a bush . . ."

"*Arf!*" She barked louder.

"I don't know why I even showed them to you," I said.

Emily stopped barking. She looked at me and said, so softly I almost couldn't hear her, "Stop doing that. It isn't funny. I love you, Sarah. And I love your poems."

Unlike in my dream, where Angel could say things like that and I knew exactly how to act, I got all flustered and emotional. So I barked. So then Emily had to bark at me again. So then I barked back at her.

"What are you *arfing* at me for?" she said. She looked so outraged, I started laughing and added a beagle howl. "You're the person putting yourself down," she said, "telling me how your poems stink."

"I know," I said, "but you're the person who had the nauseated look on her face when she was reading them."

"I was thinking about me and you," she said. "About what I'm going to do when school starts, when you have to go back to school. When I can't be with you, how it's going to be. Then I started thinking how when we go back, Monday, you could maybe come with me to Dr. Kahn?"

"I could," I said.

"We could get my ears pierced," she said. "And then we can come back here next weekend, maybe."

"We will," I said. "We're just getting started. We'll do all kinds of things." I took the poems back from her and shuffled through them. "Maybe I'll look at these again myself, later." I tucked the folder underneath my pillow. "But before we get to do any of it, I hate to remind you, they're all still downstairs. Waiting." I went to my dresser and handed her a clean T-shirt and some shorts. "The first thing we've got to do, we've got to get through breakfast."